GALLAGHER'S PRIDE

A Montana Gallagher Novel
Book One

MK MCCLINTOCK

Trappers Peak Publishing
Bigfork, Montana 59911
www.mkmcclintock.com

Publisher's Note: This is a work of fiction. Names, characters, places, and incidents are a product of the author's imagination. Locales and public names are sometimes used for atmospheric purposes. Any resemblance to actual people, living or dead, or to businesses, companies, events, institutions, or locales is completely coincidental.

2015 Large Print Paperback Edition
Published in the United States by Cambron Press.
Originally published in trade paperback by
Trappers Peak Publishing in 2012.

LARGE PRINT PAPERBACK EDITION

McClintock, MK
Gallagher's Pride; novel/MK McClintock
ISBN-13: 978-0996507608

Cover design by MK McClintock

MONTANA GALLAGHER SERIES

Gallagher's Pride
Gallagher's Hope
Gallagher's Choice
An Angel Called Gallagher
Journey to Hawk's Peak
Wild Montana Winds
The Healer of Briarwood

BRITISH AGENT NOVELS

Alaina Claiborne
Blackwood Crossing
Clayton's Honor

CROOKED CREEK SERIES

"Emma of Crooked Creek"
"Hattie of Crooked Creek"
"Briley of Crooked Creek"
"Clara of Crooked Creek"
The Women of Crooked Creek

WHITCOMB SPRINGS SERIES

"Whitcomb Springs"
"Forsaken Trail"
"Unchained Courage"

SHORT STORY COLLECTIONS

A Home for Christmas

& more to come!

To learn more about MK McClintock and her books,
please visit www.mkmcclintock.com.

For Aaron, Brett, and Nathan—the men who inspired the cowboys of Hawk's Peak.

ACKNOWLEDGMENTS

My mother provided never-ending support and assistance during the writing of this book. Thank you for always encouraging me and giving me the time from our businesses to put in the endless hours to bring the Gallaghers to life.

For my editor, Lorraine Fico-White. You've proven that no author can do it alone. Thank you for going above and beyond.

Dearest Readers,

I fell in love with the Gallagher family from their first words. The characters are flawed, likable, and yes, sometimes infuriating, but they're real and true to themselves. This is more than just a series, it's a western saga. The series follows the Gallaghers' romance, hope, and revenge over the course of several books—each one offering something new.

It should also be understood that I write fiction, not history. I do my best to stay true to the time in which the books are set, but I do take some leeway as a fiction author. I accept full responsibility for any major historical discrepancies. I hope you enjoy the story and the Gallagher family as much I do.

-MK

1

The weariness settled in not long after her ship arrived in Boston. The anger, the pain, and the betrayal still consumed her heart. The grandness of the wild territory looming ahead did nothing to assuage these feelings. It seemed so long ago that she held her father's hand as he lay dying, though barely eight months had passed. She still remembered his final words as though he'd spoken only a moment ago. "Ye're not alone in the world, me darling girl." Gazing out the train window, across the expanse of land that marked only the beginning of her journey, Brenna realized her father couldn't have foreseen where those final words would lead her.

In the countryside of Borthwick, Edinburghshire, Scotland 1869

The mare fought bravely to bring the young filly into this world, and her struggles paid off. The beautiful silver-coated filly glanced around curiously as it sought purchase on its wobbly legs. Her mother nudged the little one until it stood triumphantly and quickly sought out nourishment. The young girl on the cusp of womanhood watched with rapt attention at the miracle, then turned from the stall and raced to the main house.

"Papa! Mama! Come quickly!"

Brenna jumped up and down in the doorway of the parlor, turned around, and headed back for the stable without bothering to see if her parents followed.

Her father chuckled at the retreating girl and his wife smiled. "You did promise her a new filly."

"So I did." He laughed again and reached for his wife's hand. "Let us go and see if that's what she'll be getting."

Duncan and Rebecca Cameron walked along the green grass to the stable that had born dozens of foals and fillies over the years. Brenna had impatiently waited in great anticipation for this one day to come, for this special filly to be born. Her first horse to raise just as she chose and the most perfect gift she'd ever received.

The couple walked up and stood beside their daughter, looking over the stall door at the young filly staring curiously back at them. Brenna stood between them, and sensed their excitement nearly matched her own.

"It will be a bit of time before she can be ridden, but she's a fine-looking filly, Brenna."

"She's beautiful, Papa."

"That she is," her mother said, and placed an arm around her shoulder. "What do you say we leave her to her mother."

Brenna looked up at her father, pleading with him to let her stay out there. Her just-a-little-longer plea almost always worked when she looked at him with her small smile and wide eyes.

"Not this time, darling girl." He pulled his daughter and wife close to him and walked toward the stable entrance.

"There'll be plenty of time for ye to spend with her, but yer mother's right."

"Well, may I come out tomorrow? At sunrise?"

Her father chuckled again. "Yes, at sunrise."

Brenna knelt over the recently tilled soil, side by side with her mother. Together they sowed the flower seeds for a new garden they chose to plant near the orchard. It had always been one of her most cherished times, those hours she spent with her mother in the gardens or with her father at the stable. Few young people Brenna's age lived in their small village, but she didn't mind.

Her parents and the people who worked at Cameron Manor were her family and friends. She took her school lessons every day after she and her mother tended the gardens; her parents insisted she be educated. Her tutor, Mrs. Parks, a delightful older woman from London, spoke French and even traveled to Africa before her husband died. She encouraged Brenna to think freely and beyond the ideas written in textbooks. Brenna was delighted when her father presented her with a beautiful globe shipped from London. She spent hours asking him about his travels and how he met her mother.

Brenna remembered asking him once about her birth and if she had any other family. Her father grew quiet for a time, smiled at her, and said all the family she needed lived at Cameron Manor. He seemed so sad—she didn't ask again.

Not long after her tenth birthday, Duncan tried to teach her how to fish in one of the lakes on their estate. Brenna loved being outside, riding horses, and gardening with her mother, but she certainly didn't like worms or watching fish squiggle and squirm on the hooks. Her father seemed happy, though, so she smiled and tried not to grimace much.

Secretly she thought he knew how she felt because he didn't take her fishing again. Instead, they enjoyed long walks through the woods as he pointed out the various plants, trees, and wildlife when fortune favored them enough to catch a glimpse of a deer or fox. Her father carefully showed her the boundaries of their land so she wouldn't wander into areas where hunters may mistake her or her horse for wild game. Over the years, Brenna led a sheltered life at Cameron Manor, but she couldn't imagine spending her life anywhere else.

In the countryside of Borthwick, Edinburghshire, Scotland 1875

One week after Brenna's eighteenth birthday, on a rare spring day when the sun shone with enthusiasm, Brenna's parents hoped she would join them for a leisurely ride. Brenna's mare, Heather, enjoyed a good run that morning so she opted to ride another mount for the afternoon. Brenna often woke early to ride so her father wouldn't discover her preference to ride without a saddle. She discovered early on that though saddles offered convenience, she and Heather preferred riding without the confinement. Her mother rode one of the geldings since her mare carried another foal.

The family coveted such beautiful days. Scotland's weather could change abruptly, so they took immediate advantage of glorious weather.

An hour into their ride, a light sprinkling of rain began. Brenna thought nothing of it because the sun still shone brightly through the clouds. When the wind picked up, she turned a worried look over her shoulder toward her parents.

"We'd best head back in!" Her father's shout carried across the howling wind. "The storm'll have us soaking before long!"

Brenna turned around to answer her father, but shouting against the wind proved fruitless. She quickly closed the distance between them when a crack of thunder shuddered through the sky and frightened the animals. They started back as quickly as they could without causing injury to anyone, but another crack of thunder sounded close by and she watched as her mother's horse frightened. Rebecca couldn't calm the animal and it reared back, dropping her off the saddle before catching its leg in mud and falling over on top of her.

Duncan shouted for his wife, dismounted, and ran toward her as quickly as his legs allowed. The gelding had broken his leg and couldn't move, pinning Rebecca under its heavy mass. Brenna jumped off the mare and ran toward her parents, shielding her eyes from the pelting rain, which began to fall in earnest. She ignored the stinging pain as heavy drops made contact with her skin.

"Mama!" Brenna knelt down next to her mother's head and watched as her father tried to encourage the animal to move enough so they could pull Rebecca out from under it.

Brenna held onto her mother's cold hand and covered her with her body as best she could to shield her from the downpour.

"Brenna!" Her father looked at her and shouted over the storm. "Go, as fast as ye can and bring help."

"Papa." Brenna felt like a little girl again, uncertain what to do.

"Brenna, go! I'll stay with yer mother!" He shouted over the sounds of clapping thunder and gusting winds. "Go!"

Brenna mounted the mare and raced toward home, pleading over and over that they'd make it there without further injury so she could get help to her mother.

"Iain!" Brenna raced toward the stable, shouting Iain's name. He and his wife, Maggie, loyally served the Camerons for more than twenty years, and Brenna considered them part of the family. If anyone could help, it was Iain.

"Iain, please!" Brenna dismounted and turned, shouting his name again when he raced toward her.

"Brenna lass, whatever is wrong?"

She stood with rain-soaked hair and clothes and could not hide the panic from her eyes.

"Where are yer parents, lass?"

"Near the cliffs by Fowler's Cove." Brenna bent over, her breaths coming in short gasps. "Hurry, please. Mama's trapped under her horse."

Under different circumstances, Brenna could have admired how swiftly the older man moved into action. He rang the emergency bell by the stable door, which brought the few other servants outside. Maggie and the stable boy, who had been carrying wood inside, rushed across the grounds to the stables. Iain waited for the boy with saddled horses.

Brenna moved to remount, but Iain laid a strong hand on her shoulder.

"Stay here, lass," he said, even as she shook her head.

"I'm going."

"Ye'll hurt them more if something happened to ye. Stay."

Brenna couldn't take that risk. Iain's wife wrapped an arm around Brenna's waist, and they watched the two riders race into the storm.

Two weeks passed since the afternoon when the storm swept through and carried away bits of Brenna's heart. An accident. Everyone called it a terrible accident, but Brenna didn't want to think about it. She couldn't because her father needed her to be strong. He refused to leave Rebecca's side from the moment they finally pulled the horse off of her body. Brenna didn't have a chance to say good-bye to her mother. By the time they brought her home, she had been unconscious. When the doctor finally arrived, Rebecca had passed.

"Papa?" Brenna softly closed the door behind her as she walked into her father's study. The room remained dark, much as it had been since her mother's death. He rarely left that room and rarely ate or slept.

Brenna walked quietly over the thick rug and knelt in front of the heavy chair, where her father spent many hours. She took his hands off his lap and held them softly in her own.

"Papa?" Brenna spoke in hushed tones, but this time he lifted his eyes to hers.

"She's gone, Brenna." His voiced sounded painfully hoarse, and she pulled the blanket up higher on his chest. "Me beautiful Rebecca is gone."

"I know." Brenna held back the tears, which threatened to fall. "But she's still with us and she would not want to see you this way."

This time Duncan leaned forward and wrapped his arms around his daughter. "I know, me darling girl. I can hear her now telling me to put away me whiskey and open the windows."

"I can hear her too."

"We'll be all right, won't we, lass?"

"Yes, Papa, we'll be all right."

2

Hawk's Peak, Montana
1877

"I'm not going back."

"You're being too stubborn, Ethan. You only have one year left of college, and the ranch will still be here."

"Am I interrupting?"

Ethan turned to look at his brother who poked his head into the room.

"Yes."

"No."

Ethan Gallagher looked at his father and tried to calm himself. This stubborn streak they shared had led to a few arguments since Ethan had come of age. He loved his father and felt grateful that he was willing to share the working of the ranch with his sons. As their father told it, Jacob left the city as a young man to escape a congested life and build a legacy for his children in the West. Ethan knew his father welcomed their input when it came to ranch business, but he also knew how much Jacob Gallagher valued a solid education.

"Ethan, we can argue about this until roundup, but you're still going back."

Ethan usually kept a cool head, but he and his father shared many of the same traits. He gave his old man a good hard stare trying to decide if defying him would be worth the argument he couldn't possibly win. It galled Ethan to know that his pa was right. It galled him even more to see his brother still standing there, grinning like a fool. Knowing that Gabriel didn't have much longer before he followed in Ethan's footsteps took away some of the sting.

"All right, Pa. One more year, but after that I'm staying for good."

Jacob clasped his son's hand and gave him a smile in thanks. "One more year. Now, let's go into dinner before your mother comes in and tans us both."

Hawk's Peak Land
Outside of Briarwood, Montana
Territory
1879

He couldn't let the grievance go unanswered. His parents found thirty years of peaceful living in this beautiful and rugged land. They traveled to the northern territories to escape the sweltering madness of Texas, worked hard, and found peace. Even when the land became the Territory of Montana more than ten years ago, they lived in peace with the other settlers swarming the West to mine and graze cattle. In all that time, they had only one encounter with the Indians when they crossed the Gallaghers' land to reach their own. Since the army met defeat by some of the tribes about ten years back, the Indians were content to keep peace as long as the settlers stayed on their land and left the natives alone on theirs.

Peace for the Gallaghers had ended with Nathan Hunter.

The blackguard purchased land only a few miles from their extensive borders. The small stretch of grass between the two spreads belonged to a belligerent old swindler, Dwight Dickens, who refused to work the valuable land. When he realized more than one interested party coveted the land, he let the bidding war begin. With little more than fifteen acres, the land didn't offer much except the water. Water and grass were the greatest currencies out west, without which a rancher may as well pack up and leave. Control of that stretch meant control of the stream coming down from the mountains. The snowfall each year assured that the water flowed continuously through till the next winter and kept their ponds full.

The Gallaghers won the bidding war, but only once they agreed that Old Man Dickens could keep his small homestead on the land. A small sacrifice for the water rights.

One week later, Nathan Hunter's men stretched barbed wire along the new boundary line. The Gallaghers hated wire.

When they first arrived in Montana Territory, the area consisted of a few small ranches in the area that they chose to settle, a day's ride north of Bozeman. Not many settlers lasted past their first winter in the harsh climate, but the Gallaghers found home and soon became one of the most respected ranching families in the territory. Known for their fairness in business and hard work, they made a solid name for themselves. Jacob Gallagher built a legacy on that wild land, and his children were damned if they'd let one man destroy it.

Ethan Gallagher sat tall atop the midnight black stallion, a magnificent animal bred from the Hawk's Peak bloodline. Gabriel, his younger brother by two years, sat just as tall on his own dark Thoroughbred, a beauty he brought with him to Montana from a Kentucky horse farm on his way back from school in the East. Both animals wore the staggered HP brand of the Hawk's Peak ranch.

Gabriel swore loudly enough to draw a glance from his brother. He settled the animal with a soothing word. Ethan said nothing. He appeared to not have a care in the world. Gabriel knew better. Ethan didn't wear his anger on the surface. The darkness of his eyes and the clenched jaw were sure indications that his brother could commit murder. In this instance, it would be the murder of Nathan Hunter. Gabriel wouldn't think ill of his brother if it came to that end.

When the wranglers went out to round up a few strays that had wandered during a fierce thunderstorm the previous night, they discovered the latest in a string of misdeeds. A cow lay dead on the earth, its blood mixing with the summer grass and its eyes open and lifeless. The cow dropped a calf only the week before. The calf had been injured trying to stay near its mother, but when the wranglers brought it back to the ranch, everyone knew they couldn't save him.

Ethan's gaze went to the mangled legs of

the animal, sure indications that the innocent creature struggled and suffered before death and had been unsuccessful in its fight to survive. The deadly wire wrapped around the poor creature's legs left enough proof for Ethan. Proof that regardless of the backbreaking rail fence the Gallaghers put up to keep their cattle from that particular stretch of wire, someone deliberately put the wire onto their land.

Only one of many unprovable incidences which had occurred since the arrival of Nathan Hunter. Ethan was close to not caring about proof for the marshal. If the law of the territory couldn't put a stop to it, the law of the land would. Ethan spared his brother one last look, turned his mount, and headed for the bordering spread.

In the countryside of Borthwick, Edinburghshire, Scotland February 1882

"Papa?" The hands firmly within Brenna's

grasp felt as cold as the frigid lochs in winter. Her emerald-green eyes, a gift from her mother, gazed into the haggard face of the only man she ever loved.

"Me darling Brenna." His voice sounded hoarse and the strength behind his deep brogue weakened.

"Yes, Papa, I'm here."

"I must . . ."

"You must rest now, Papa."

"No, I must tell ye." He breathed in as much air into his lungs as he could. When he spoke again, his voice came out surprisingly smooth and his eyes weary with the weight of secrets long kept. Brenna sat up straighter, and held tightly to her father's weakened hand. She waited for him to find his words.

"Many years ago, I traveled to America. I ended up in Texas where I met yer mother."

Brenna knew of how her parents met, but she waited and listened.

His eyes filled with determination as though these last words would be the most important he'd ever speak. "Yer mother and I fell in love immediately. I knew the moment we met that we'd marry. I would have done anything to make her mine Brenna. Anything. Her father dinna want the marriage and dinna want me near me Rebecca. Yer mother defied him and we married without his blessing. When he discovered her rebellion, he disowned her and told her never to return. Yer mother never wept for the loss. She packed her things and we left on the next train heading east and then a ship home to Scotland. We told ye yer grandfather died before ye were born." Her father coughed and once again struggled with his breathing while the sickness consumed his lungs.

The great man Brenna loved and revered her whole life was not the man slipping away before her eyes. She feared what he would say next, but waited even as the weight of grief settled in her heart. He asked her to pull open the drawer next to his bed. Her hands wanted to tremble, but she didn't allow herself that weakness. Brenna pulled an opened envelope from the drawer. The crispness of the paper had long since faded into worn softness indicating how often the words had been read. It was addressed to her mother, postmarked Texas.

His breathing became more shallow. "Yer mother and I agreed not to tell ye, but now I'm thinking that we did ye wrong lass. We never thought we wadna be here to protect ye." He took another labored breath and in a voice barely above a whisper said, "Yer grandfather lives. He's an unkind man and he . . . but ye're not alone in the world, me darling girl."

Duncan Cameron struggled to bring air into his lungs, and it became evident that the loving father who taught her to ride horses as a child would soon leave her. He didn't have many breaths left in his once strong and proud body. Yet even now, his words pulled at something within her that she couldn't explain. Brenna wanted to ask her father from what they wanted to protect her. Now she could ask him nothing. His eyes closed and soon after, his soul left his silent body and departed the earth.

Brenna never felt more alone. The pain his passing left behind soon festered into hatred. She never hated anyone before and didn't think she possessed the capacity for it. Then she read her grandfather's letter to her mother.

October 1857
Rebecca,
I have received your letter and will write only this once. I have not changed my feelings in regard to your scandalous marriage to that Scotsman or for your disregard to my orders that you not marry. Your mother is in agreement. You wrote to tell me of your children. Know only this. Before you left I told you what I wanted, and I expect you to heed my wishes.
Nathan Hunter

Brenna did not know why her parents kept the letter after all these years. Even after her mother passed on, her father kept it hidden. Duncan Cameron died before he could explain why Nathan Hunter spoke of scandal or why he hated her father so much. Brenna's mind filled with questions. What did my mother take? What of my grandmother? Did she still live? Papa didn't mention a grandmother. He said only that I wasn't alone, but he couldn't possibly mean my grandfather.

Even more troubling was the mention of children. She was an only child. Her father had left her with too many unanswered questions.

Only one choice remained. She knew Iain would never understand. Maggie would insist on going or at the very least, hiring a companion. Brenna didn't want to share what she believed had to be done with anyone, especially a stranger, and she couldn't ask Maggie to leave her husband and home. Brenna didn't know when she would again step foot on Scottish soil. The thought of telling them pained her, but she owed them the truth . . . or most of it. She would promise to hire someone to accompany her, but only until she reached the ship. By that time, it would be too late for anyone to stop her.

3

Briarwood, Montana Territory
October 1882

It seemed almost impossible that Brenna now stood in the middle of a dusty street on a brisk autumn morning thousands of miles from everything she knew and treasured. But there she stood in the town of Briarwood in Montana Territory. The arduous journey left her weary and homesick: the seemingly never-ending crossing of the Atlantic, the miles of train tracks, the stink of unwashed people the farther from civilization she got, and the rattling stage ride. But this is where her grandfather lived or so the telegrams she received from the private investigator had indicated.

It had not taken long to discover the whereabouts of Nathan Hunter. Once Brenna arrived on Boston's soil, a place so foreign to the country she loved, she had sent telegrams to the postmarked address in Texas from where Nathan Hunter's last letter was sent. A reply arrived less than two days later informing her that Nathan Hunter no longer lived in Texas. He had moved to the Montana Territory some years back. With a dozen more telegrams and the services of a costly private detective, she found him.

If Brenna's mind had not been filled with questions and worries, perhaps she could have appreciated the grandeur of the place where she now stood. Mountains higher than she'd ever imagined jutted upward from the earth. Those in Scotland stood as mere hills compared to the towering peaks surrounding the valley, which seemed to stretch farther than she could see. The fresh pine-scented air reminded her of the long walks she used to take with her father back home, when she picked bundles of heather for her mother. There seemed to be no end to the journey an eagle could take in the vast blue skies. Wildness and beauty unlike anything she'd ever imagined surrounded her.

Unfortunately this majesty was wasted on Brenna those first moments. She held her reticule close to her bosom, thinking of the letters tucked safely inside. She had found two more missives when she went through her father's belongings. Neither told her anything more about Nathan Hunter than what she already surmised. She detested the man and the facts began to support her feelings. Her hatred still lurked below the surface, even though she knew it likely hurt her more than him.

Brenna didn't need to look at the letters. She had memorized their content on the sea crossing. Those worn papers gave her a small measure of courage, misplaced though it seemed right now.

Many times on the journey here, she questioned her decision to leave behind her beloved Scotland to find this man who destroyed his family. Of course her mother had been happy. Rebecca loved Duncan

Cameron more than life itself, but the kindest part of her soul still believed that her own father could someday soften his heart. Brenna learned something about her mother in those letters. Rebecca Cameron had possessed one of the most forgiving hearts she'd ever known a person to have.

Brenna had no intention of trying to spark a family relationship with Nathan Hunter, but her stubborn nature refused to let the matter of the letter's content go without answers. The most puzzling thing of all was the mysterious item that he claimed his daughter took from him. The other two letters spoke of nothing but that, though bereft of details.

With a deep sigh, Brenna set those thoughts aside as practicality weighed in. She must learn her way around this foreign place and find accommodations for her duration. Reports indicated that the territory was a hard land, and her solicitor used every last bit of persuasion to convince her not to go. Brenna's determination won, though she was grateful at least one person knew where she'd gone.

The crisp wind blew across the grass-covered valley and caressed Brenna's face. She pulled the fine, wool scarf, the last Christmas gift from her mother, tighter around her neck and shoulders. Her long, heavy, wool coat kept the rest of her warm enough. Although, she admitted to herself that it wasn't the weather that brought on a sudden chill. Twenty-five years of Scottish winters made her impervious to the cool breezes she encountered in this country. The chill came from fear.

Fear unlike any she'd known in her life consumed her. Through the length of her journey here, she had been only angry and saddened about leaving home. Fear didn't have a chance to settle into her mind until she faced the stark reality of what she'd done. She had plenty of money to survive and even start a new life here if she chose. Her parents provided well for her, though some of that remained a mystery to her. The funds she now carried in her reticule had been tucked securely at a bank in

Boston. Brenna's only clue had been a bank draft found among her father's papers in his study and later confirmed by his solicitor.

The other passengers alighted from the stagecoach, though her thoughts were not on them either. Nor did she notice at first the damp dirt on which she stood.

One man watched from the door of the general store. It seemed as though every day new folks made their way north. Some for opportunity, others for adventure, and some to find peace. He could usually tell by the looks of a person what brought them, and it didn't take long to tell which ones would be hightailing it back to wherever they came from once they'd had a taste of winter. Most of the men and women appeared to be well-seasoned to frontier life—except one. He stepped away from the general store and slowly made his way across the street to get a better look at a beauty he was certain fell into the group of those who couldn't possibly handle life in his wilderness.

Brenna took in her surroundings.

Briarwood appeared to be exactly what replies to her inquiries reported—a small settlement content to grow at its own pace, with wide streets and a good-sized general store located next to a barber shop. Another large building, void of sign but well-tended, stood to the other side. Down the street near the livery, a medical clinic sign hung from the doctor's office. The hotel saloon, where she had been dropped off, was across from the general store and appeared clean enough, but she cringed at the thought of sleeping in a saloon and decided she'd find other accommodations.

A dressmaker's shop with simple versions of the latest fashions stood next to a small bank bearing a clock above the sign. A café and quaint newspaper and telegraph office were nearby. Farther down, a few houses lined the street, and in the distance a proud white church had been erected next to a well-kept churchyard. A small red schoolhouse was located off to the other side of a meadow near the church. It appeared to be freshly painted. Despite the population growing in the southern part of the territory, Briarwood seemed to move to its own rhythm. Ignoring the faster progress of other towns, the peacefulness of this settlement reminded Brenna of home. She held back the tears and replaced them with the determination that brought her this far.

Brenna watched as the stagecoach drove away and left a cloud of dust in its wake. Her gaze followed the last link to the life she left behind as the rambling transportation disappeared across the land. In her mind, there was no turning back until she found the answers she desperately sought.

Brenna picked up her small valise and noticed that the driver had left her trunks on the side of the road. Taking yet another deep breath, she turned and then nearly collapsed.

"What in darnation did you think you were doing, Riley?" The angry bellow followed a scrawny man who nearly aided Brenna in her fall to the sludge below.

A strong pair of hands caught her from

behind and pulled her quickly back to the boardwalk. Forgetting those hands for the moment, Brenna watched the man she assumed was Riley fall face first and consume a mouthful of the grimed street in the process. A disturbing and apparently angry man pushed open the swinging doors and stormed out to the street. Riley picked himself up off of the ground before the goliath could kick him in the ribs, which is where his booted foot almost landed.

"That's right. You run off now and don't let me catch you back in here until you're old enough to drink and whore."

A small crowd gathered around and a few unapproved glances shot toward the rangy and unfortunate-looking man who had just shouted. He yelled at the onlookers who then dispersed and went about their business. Brenna stood there, not knowing what to think about the people of this new land. She had witnessed a brawl once in their village, unbeknownst to her overprotective parents, but these people appeared to be open about it. And she had heard people call the Highlanders barbarians.

Brenna also found herself fascinated and couldn't step away. The same disturbing man who had thrown the smaller man he called Riley onto the street, took off his hat and slapped it against his thigh a few times, transferring dust from his pants to his hat, before he turned and noticed her. A small smile formed on his mouth, showing the barest hint of crooked teeth. Brenna shuddered at the uncomfortable, and unwelcome, way his eyes roamed freely up and down her body. She felt exposed, despite all of the fabric she wore.

"Howdy, ma'am." The stranger approached her. "My name is Bradford James and it's sure a pleasure to make your acquaintance."

Brenna wished for an escape, and her heart nearly leapt in her chest at the sound of the deep, smooth voice coming from directly behind her.

"Quite a show you've put on for us today, James."

Brenna saw the subtle change come over

Mr. James and almost feared looking behind her. The strong hands. She now remembered them pulling her to safety. She would bet anything that those hands belonged to the man who seemed to be the cause of Mr. James's angry discomfort.

"Now, Gallagher, this ain't any of your concern. Just a little family disagreement." Bradford then turned his attention back to Brenna. "I didn't catch your name, ma'am."

"She didn't give it."

Goodness, that voice could scare the fierce Scottish winds off of their current. Brenna had never remained quiet for so long, but she willingly deferred this particular argument to her mysterious protector. She kept her peace and waited.

Bradford looked at Ethan and then back at Brenna. Brenna nervously tucked her red hair into her hat and prayed she wasn't about to witness an altercation between the two men. Bradford James eventually tipped his hat and sauntered back into the saloon.

Brenna let out a slow, quiet breath,

grateful that Mr. James had departed. Everything about that man made her wish she had quick access to a bath. Remembering why the stranger had made himself scarce, Brenna slowly turned around and stared into a wide chest covered in a clean black shirt and dusty coat. She titled her head up, her eyes following a path that reached nearly a foot above her, and found a grin. She stared into the most beautiful blue eyes ever to be found on a man—not even a regular blue. They looked almost gray, but dark, like the night sky when the moon shone. His dark brown hair escaped from under the wide-brimmed hat she'd seen wear in the West. His face didn't appear to have met a razor in a few days. The result should have made him look unkempt, but instead he exhibited danger. The high cheek bones and square jaw combined with those dark eyes were magnified by his deeply tanned skin. Obviously her rescuer—a cowboy a gentleman on the train would have called him—didn't always wear his hat.

"Not exactly a place for a lady to be

standing on her own." The man's smooth drawl sent a shiver through her body.

"Yes, I realize that, sir, but the stage stopped here, so this is where I stand." Subtlety and patience were two traits she did not possess, and she needed to find a hotel. "I don't suppose you know of a Nathan Hunter residing in the area?"

The grin slowly faded and those grayish-blue midnight-colored eyes became darker, if that was possible.

"Yes, he lives around here." The cowboy's voice hardened.

She found that curious, but the relief that coursed through Brenna couldn't trample the anger still festering deep within her breast for the man she sought out.

"Would you happen to know where he lives?"

It appeared to Brenna that he didn't want to answer her, and his eyes took on a dangerous glint.

"Now, what would you want with Nathan Hunter?"

Brenna didn't know what about this man

~ 38 ~

riled her more—the tone of his voice or the chilled look in his eyes.

"I do appreciate your help, sir, with my near tumble, but I don't see how that is any concern of yours."

After a moment he still hadn't answered.

"He's my grandfather, if you must know."

Ethan didn't think he could be more shocked if his brother walked down the streets of Briarwood naked. He studied the woman from head to toe, much like Bradford James had done, but with different intent. He couldn't tell much about her body as she kept it well covered in expensive blue wool and a deep-green scarf. She stood about a foot shorter than his six feet four, and he'd guess that she was nice and curvy underneath that coat. He did notice her hair—a deep, dark, flaming red under a midnight-blue hat. Her expressive eyes, as green as the summer pastures out at the ranch, were surrounded by creamy white skin that looked to have been well guarded from the sun. He couldn't fault James for admiring the shiny penny newly arrived, but out west that could mean trouble and it didn't mean he liked it.

Brenna found herself growing impatient as this man boldly studied her, though she had to admit that it didn't bother her. Mr. James's perusal disgusted her—this one merely irritated her. She grew impatient because after months of travel she was so close to finding her grandfather and this man wanted to gawk.

Finally he spoke. "The Double Bar is north of here. That's Hunter's spread, though I wasn't aware of him having any relations still around here."

"Well, I haven't exactly met him before." *What business was it of this man's anyway?* If she wanted to be truthful with herself, it could be that from the moment she looked into those fascinating eyes and grinning face, she wanted to trust him. Brenna knew it could just be weariness from her travels, and she didn't need to be making mistakes. The journey had been difficult enough convincing men she wasn't alone. Brenna had even gone so far as to wear one of her mother's old rings over the glove on her left hand. Whether others had thought her married or a widow, she didn't care as long as they left her alone.

The stranger offered a sardonic raising of his eyebrow, which plainly told Brenna that the man thought she was daft.

Ethan most definitely thought Brenna was in over her head. He'd just as soon see the woman right back on the next stage out of there. In the meantime, he didn't want to take her out to the old man's place without more information. It didn't matter that she obviously possessed gumption; he couldn't risk it. Hell, he thought, I'd try to keep a stray dog from the hands of that man. For reasons he couldn't fathom, he just appointed himself her protector, and he didn't even know her name.

"Well, I can certainly show you the way to the Double Bar, but you may want to stay in town for a couple of nights until you've had a chance to actually meet Hunter."

"Thank you, sir, but I have no intention of staying with Nathan Hunter. If you could point me toward accommodations in town, I would be grateful."

As an afterthought, Brenna stuck out her hand. "It seems I've forgotten my manners. Brenna Cameron."

The man raised that infernal brow and stared at her hand, but he accepted it. "Ethan Gallagher."

"A pleasure to meet you, Mr. Gallagher."

In answer to her question, Ethan was about to point her across the street to Widow Dawson's Boarding House but Bradford James chose that moment to saunter back out of the saloon.

"Well, well. It don't appear you've gone far, Gallagher." He tipped his hat to Brenna and smiled, showing discolored teeth.

"I could say the same for you, Bradford." His smooth, deep voice took on a sharp tone.

Brenna wondered why these two seemed at such odds but decided to once again keep silent. She wasn't in such desperate need of friends that she would be willing to shake hands with Mr. James.

Bradford lost his smile. He ignored Ethan and turned his attention back to Brenna.

The idiotic sop was obviously intoxicated, Brenna thought.

"Ma'am, I'd be happy to escort you to your destination." He slurred his words, even as he held out his arm for her.

Brenna forced herself not to cringe openly and decided to break her silence. She didn't have time for the lout or his ridiculous advances. "That won't be necessary, sir, but I thank you for the gesture." She hoped that would be the end of it, and in polite society it should have been.

"Now, ma'am, it ain't safe for a lady like yerself to be walking around alone."

"Be that as it may, sir, I am quite capable and as you can see, in good hands." Brenna gestured toward Ethan, hoping he would forgive her boldness and go along with her deception. The dark look that came over Mr. James didn't reassure her.

"She's with you, Gallagher?"

"She is."

Ethan said nothing more, and Brenna slowly released the breath she didn't realized she'd been holding. She did that a lot lately.

"Well now ain't that sweet. I hadn't taken her for the type, but I guess you never can tell," Bradford said with a beastly laugh, too drunk to keep quiet.

Another equally ugly man—she hadn't expected so many in one town—appeared to be a friend to the drunk, although he hit Bradford in the ribs and told him to shut up.

Ethan ignored the other man and stepped around Brenna, blocking her view of Bradford as he spoke with him. "And what type would that be?" His smooth voice sounded colder and harder.

Brenna worried that she might have caused what could turn into an unpleasant altercation. She gently laid a soft hand on Ethan's arm, hoping to gain his attention. He ignored her. She found that annoying.

"The type to bed down with the likes of

you, Gallagher, but with all of that money, she probably just shuts her eyes."

Brenna cringed at the sickening laugh, but not nearly as much as the sound of a fist hitting bone and the blood that appeared all over Mr. James's face. Oddly, the crude comment about her being a whore didn't bother her and she easily discarded it from her mind.

"You're having all of the fun without me again, Ethan?"

Brenna turned to see another man closer to her age with dark brown hair and an easy smile. There could be no mistaking where those eyes came from. This one looked just as handsome as Ethan, and Brenna had no doubt they were related.

Ethan waited a moment to be sure that Bradford would stay on the ground. "No, you're just late as usual." Ethan offered the younger man a genuine smile. "Are you finished up at the livery?"

His brother merely nodded as his attention focused on Brenna. "The name is Gabriel Gallagher, ma'am, and it is indeed a pleasure." The grin on the man's face brought one to Brenna's, and she found herself delighted with his charm.

"I am Brenna Cameron, Mr. Gallagher."

"Please, it's Gabriel."

"Very well, Gabriel. Your brother kindly came to my aid with a certain . . . mishap."

Ethan arched a brow at her as he looked back at Bradford being carted away to the doc by two of his equally inebriated friends. He half wondered how a genteel woman did no more than slightly shudder at what just took place.

Gabriel lifted his own brow in mocking laughter. "Yes, well, Ethan is our local rescuer of damsels in distress."

Ethan rolled his eyes at his brother.

Brenna laughed. "Well I assure you that I am no longer in distress and merely here to visit . . . uh family."

"I know pretty much everyone in these parts, though no Camerons. Who might your family be?"

Brenna wondered if others felt the same way about her grandfather.

"Nathan Hunter."

Ethan watched as the smile and charm

left his brother's chiseled face and waited for the smoldering ball of fury to erupt as it usually did when Hunter's name was mentioned. He knew Gabriel wouldn't take his anger out on a woman, but his hatred ran deep, like all of theirs.

"I wasn't aware of old Hunter still having any kin." Gabriel's words came out strained.

Now why does everyone keep saying that? wondered Brenna.

"Yes, well, he does. Now if you'll excuse me, gentlemen, I really should procure myself a room for the evening." She turned to Ethan. "I do thank you for your assistance."

Just as she was about to walk onto the street, a strong hand once again grabbed her from behind. Brenna turned and looked up into those dark eyes. She wasn't used to being handled so casually or with such strength. No man of her acquaintance could compare to the ones they bred out here.

"It would be best if you didn't stay in town tonight, Miss Cameron."

"And why is that?"

"I guarantee that bad element is just waiting to find you alone, and Widow Dawson is hardly suitable protection."

"And what exactly are you suggesting, sir? The saloon?"

"Yes, what are you suggesting, Ethan?" Gabriel lost his smile, and Brenna regretted that.

Ethan shot his brother a dark look and turned back to those waiting green eyes.

Damn. In the deepest part of his gut, Ethan knew he couldn't just shrug this woman off and send her on her way. He felt protective of all women, as did his brother. They just couldn't stand by and watch a woman being mistreated, whether it was their business or not. This, however, seemed to be something more. A part of Ethan that he had believed died long ago also told him not to let this new arrival get away. He tried ignoring it, but duty came first and it was only Miss Cameron's safety he had in mind. At least that's what he kept telling himself.

"You'll come home with us."

4

"Are you out of your mind?" The words tumbled from her mouth before she could stop them, but he truly shocked her.

"No, actually I'm not. It's your safety I'm thinking of." Ethan loosened the hold on her arm.

Brenna let out an exasperated sigh, something her mother had always tried to discourage. "I do appreciate your kindness, Mr. Gallagher—"

"Ethan."

"Ethan, but I'm certainly not the type of woman to just go home with two men whether I know them or not. It would be highly inappropriate, not to mention stupid."

"And you're not stupid."

"Not as far as I can tell." Brenna rarely took offense to what people said, too comfortable in her own skin to care, but this man riled her and he did it effortlessly.

"Miss Cameron, I have to agree with Ethan. Bradford isn't the type of man you'd want to tangle with."

"Oh, and you and your brother are?" Brenna stared up at Ethan's brother, uncertain why he seemed amused, and became distracted by his smile. *If one man could manage clean teeth, what happened to the rest of the men in town?* she asked herself.

"I assure you that there is nothing improper about it. Hawk's Peak is a large spread with a lot of people including our sister, and Mabel, our housekeeper." Gabriel offered assurance since his brother continued to keep silent.

Brenna looked at both men and considered her options. *This is not how it was supposed to turn out.* In the short time since her arrival, Brenna had witnessed a fight in broad daylight, made an enemy out of that disgusting Mr. James, met two of the most handsome men she had ever seen, found the location of Nathan Hunter, and now entertained going home with two complete strangers. She hadn't even left the steps of the hotel saloon.

"Very well, I'll go, but only because I'm tired of standing here. I have no desire to meet up with Mr. James again, and you offered to point the way to Nathan Hunter's ranch."

Gabriel looked quickly at his brother, but Ethan just shook his head to keep him quiet.

Brenna missed the exchange and motioned to her trunks. "I don't suppose there's a place in town to store these."

The brothers looked down at the four large trunks sitting in the street where the stage driver left her baggage.

"Were you planning on staying long?" Gabriel grinned.

Brenna however was quite serious when she answered, "As long as it takes."

Ethan nodded to Gabriel as he loaded

the trunks into a large brown wagon
Brenna hadn't noticed before, being led by
two exceptional creatures. She knew
horseflesh and these animals were
magnificent. Ethan led her over to the
front and helped her up to the buckboard
bench.

Once the men loaded the trunks into the
wagon, already filled with supplies,
Gabriel untied a tall brown gelding from
the hitching post and mounted the animal
as though born in a saddle. Ethan settled
himself into the seat beside Brenna and
took up the reins. He stared at her for a
moment and then shook his head as
though to himself. "Welcome to Montana,
Miss Cameron."

He slapped the reins and Brenna
watched the clapboard buildings grow
smaller and smaller as they left Briarwood
behind them. She wondered, as she lost
sight of the town, what she had gotten
herself into.

The three travelers remained silent
during the ride to Hawk's Peak. The
beautiful countryside had Brenna

thinking of her own Scotland. The peaks looming above them certainly stood grander than her Scottish hills, and she had never seen a sky such a magnificent blue. A sky so spacious there seemed to be no end and no beginning. A flock of geese flew high above them on an invisible path in that wide expanse of blue. The pine-scented air carried with it the promise of cold, the kind of cold that made a person wish for a warm hearth and woolen blankets.

Aye, a beautiful place I've come to, she thought, *though my heart still aches for home.* But, this could very well be her home now. Brenna knowingly made that decision months ago when she first planned the journey, having decided failure was not an option, even if it took her a lifetime. Then again, Brenna didn't believe she'd find patience anytime soon. A lifetime was too long to wait.

Sometime later, as the sun began to set over the mountains, Brenna sighted something in the distance. When they rode a little farther, she could make out an expansive and impressive timber and stone house, its size shaming some of the homes she had seen back east. Her own Cameron Manor, built a century ago and made of Scotland's strong stone, had stood proudly through many generations. This home of the Gallaghers was no less impressive. She recognized the good workmanship. Only someone who built something to last went to the great expense to build a home like this in the middle of God's open country.

Another smaller house, similar in design, came into view as did a large barn and stable and various other outbuildings, all built in the same wood and stone as the main house. It was a beautiful ranch, especially in the light of the setting sun with the backdrop of purple and gold-tinted mountain peaks.

She then noticed the gardens. Glorious blooms holding on to life in the autumn air, towered above the fence stretching around the house. Only a woman's touch could create such beauty in this wilderness, she thought with some relief.

Then another thought occurred to her, and she addressed her question to no one in particular. "Is your family going to mind that I've come here? Or are you in the habit of bringing home strange women who ride in on the stage?"

Ethan pulled the team to a stop in front of the long, timber hitching rail and looked at Brenna. There was just something about this woman that seemed to drive him a bit insane. He saw fear in her eyes— he couldn't miss the subtle emotion—but she also exuded strength. Her strength brought her to a foreign land and like it or not, into his life. He just wanted to put her up for the night, show her the way to Hunter's spread, and be done with her. Even as he thought it, he knew he was lying to himself.

"You'll be welcome here." It was all he'd offer.

Brenna decided that perhaps she could simply pay for her room and board for the night. Feeling better about intruding on the unsuspecting family, she let Ethan help her down from the wagon. The unsettled feeling within crept up once more and then disappeared when he let go of her waist.

She was about to ask about his family when a horse and rider cantered up with what appeared to be a wolf following close behind.

"It's about time you returned. We thought you'd decided to stay in town tonight."

Brenna saw Ethan's face light up and turned to see the person who brought out such a reaction in the stoic man. Brenna was surprised to see a rumpled, but pretty young woman sitting atop an equally pretty white mare. She wore a dusty blue blouse and dark-brown riding skirt with well-worn boots and a bright crimson cloth tied around her neck. She appeared to be only a few years younger than Brenna. Her slightly tan skin emphasized her sharp features, as though she had just been kissed by the afternoon sun. The rich brown hair and startling blue eyes claimed her as a Gallagher. Brenna felt an odd sense of relief knowing that this woman must be their sister.

The younger woman's gaze wandered over to settle on Brenna. Brenna could feel those midnight-blue eyes boring into her. She stood her ground wishing that she had stayed in town because those eyes seemed to reach deep inside to secrets she wished to remain hidden. The brothers just waited, keeping their silence. Brenna was about to introduce herself when the younger woman jumped down from her mare and walked over. The wolf, or whatever it was, sauntered up to stand next to the woman and accept a gentle pat on the head from Ethan. The woman held out her hand, startling Brenna, and offered a genuine smile.

"I'm Eliza Gallagher. Welcome to Hawk's Peak."

Brenna automatically took the offered hand. "Brenna Cameron, a pleasure to meet you."

Eliza arched a brow. The entire family seemed to have that gesture down. She smiled. "I like your accent. What brings you all the way to Montana Territory?"

"I'm here to see my grandfather and your brother kindly offered his assistance."

"Well that was certainly kind of Ethan," she said, a bit sarcastically, causing Brenna to wonder why she didn't say Gabriel. Eliza took a sidelong glance at her older brother, but said nothing to him.

Turning back to Brenna she asked, "Who's your grandfather?"

"I think it's time we get this wagon unloaded and Miss Cameron inside. It's a wonder that Mabel hasn't come storming out the front door yet." He offered both Brenna and his sister a half-smile and scooted Eliza away.

Wondering what Ethan was about, Brenna watched him urge his sister back to her horse. Eliza remounted and rode beside Gabriel to the barn.

"I don't suppose you'll tell me that your sister will care about my grandfather's name?"

Ethan removed his hat and ran a hand through his thick, wavy hair. "No, I won't tell you that."

"Then will you tell me why?"

"We'd better get you inside now. I'll have one of the boys bring your trunks in." Ethan wasn't subtle about his desire not to answer her question.

Brenna let it go for the time being. "That's really not necessary. I only plan on staying tonight."

Ethan ignored her with another smile. He had wonderfully full lips for a man. Mentally shaking herself, and realizing that further conversation with him was futile, Brenna walked beside Ethan up the cut stone walk to the expansive porch that went from one end of the front to the other and wrapped around to the side and back of the house. The family quite obviously prospered in this wilderness, and she could only imagine the hard work it would have taken to build their ranch.

The front door opened just as Ethan reached for the handle, and Brenna found herself looking into one of the kindest faces she had ever seen.

"Well, Lordy Ethan. It's about time you brought home a pretty young lady!"

The boisterous voice and bright toothy grin immediately put Brenna at ease. Before she could correct the other woman, Ethan changed before her eyes and gave the older woman the biggest grin she'd ever seen on a man. This man's moods changed as swiftly as the Scottish weather.

"Well how about letting us inside, Mabel, so we can get some of that heavenly food I smell?"

Mabel studied him with the discerning look she gave any of them when she wasn't going to let a subject drop, but she smiled and held her own counsel, much to Ethan's relief. She stepped aside and held the door wide so they could pass, but stopped Gabriel and Eliza before they could enter the house.

"Now you two just go on around back through the kitchen and get that dust off before you go traipsing across my clean floor. You both look as though you've been wrestling steers."

Since brother and sister refused to make eye contact and did in fact look like they'd been wrestling something, they mumbled on their way out. Ethan decided not to bother asking what they had been doing, though he'd bet his sister won. Remembering his manners, which he seemed to be forgetting a lot today, he introduced the two women.

"Mabel darling, this is Brenna Cameron. She just came in on today's stage and since there weren't appropriate accommodations in town, she'll be staying here for a few days. Miss Cameron, this is Mabel."

Brenna wanted to once again correct Ethan but wasn't given the chance.

Mabel raised both brows at Ethan and turned her attention to Brenna. "It's nice to meet you, Miss Cameron."

"Please, it's Brenna. A pleasure to meet you, Mabel." Brenna opted to go along with the older woman's misconceptions and let Ethan say what he wanted. She would address his high-handed behavior later.

"Well then, why don't you follow me and we'll get you settled."

Brenna moved in behind Mabel and

listened to her say something about baggage. Brenna was too occupied looking around to pay attention.

The spacious front hall boasted rafters high in the ceiling and took up a large amount of area. Furnishings as fine as anything she'd seen in Europe were situated comfortably throughout the room. Heavy curtains draped tall windows, creating an elegant frame for the majestic view of the mountains beyond. The stairs she now climbed smelled of beeswax from a recent polishing. The walls were covered with beautiful paintings of varying geographical origins.

One near the top stopped her and her eyes misted. Home. Scotland. Brenna recognized the Highlands she often visited with her father, and memories flooded her heart.

"Is everything all right, dear?"

Brenna turned abruptly and looked to the landing where Mabel waited, eyes curious.

"Oh yes, I'm sorry to have kept you." Brenna cleared her throat and climbed to the landing. She followed Mabel down the long carpeted hallway and into a spacious and beautifully furnished bedroom, lighter in tones than the rest of the house but the richness of foreign furnishings extended here. A large four poster iron bed covered in heavy quilts and feather ticking consumed one third of the room, and yet ample space remained for a wardrobe, a welcoming settee next to a tall stone fireplace, and a writing desk placed just below one of the windows. The sun barely floated into the room as the evening hour descended.

Though rustic, the house wasn't at all what she expected to find out in this wilderness. Even Mabel sounded as though she hailed from the East, her accent like some of those Brenna heard on the train journey here.

I wonder how she came to be here? thought Brenna.

"You'll be comfortable in here." Mabel walked across the room to spread the curtains open. "I'll send someone up with a bath for you to freshen up and then I'll

bring up a tray of food. I imagine you're
tired from the journey."

Brenna nodded, absently thanked the
woman. She walked back over to the bed,
sat down, and wondered what came next.
Brenna had always been strong, and her
mother used to say that her strength
would be a blessing and a curse. Brenna
knew only that strength carried her
through her grief, kept her from tears
through her long voyage, and helped her
to stand up against everything unpleasant
that happened on the journey here. The
strength she had nursed and prided
herself on over the years wanted to take a
back seat to grief. Looking around at the
beautiful room and seeing only
strangeness, Brenna lay down on the
heavy white quilts of the bed and
succumbed to the tears she desperately
had kept at bay.

"I don't suppose you'll tell me why you
brought that young lady home?"

Ethan turned away from the pot of stew
he had been about to sample and leaned

against the counter. Mabel wore a no-nonsense look and stepped over to take the spoon from Ethan's hand. She was the only woman alive who could get away with telling any one of the Gallaghers exactly what she thought, and Mabel often had a lot on her mind. A boisterous woman originally from Georgia by way of Philadelphia, she had seen her fair share of a hard life, but she survived and found her way up to Montana when Ethan was still a young boy. Mabel was a survivor with a kind heart, and she became a member of the family the day the children's mother took her in.

Ethan loved this woman as he did any other member of his family, but in moments such as this, he wished she didn't know him so well. "I happened to be there when the stage dropped her off. Unfortunately, so was Bradford James."

Mabel's lips became a straight line and her eyes narrowed when she heard the name.

"Anyway, he noticed her right off and looked to cause trouble. So, we brought her here."

Mabel obviously didn't think that was the whole story. "Is she just in town for a visit or did you plan on keeping her?"

"She's here looking for her kin." He hoped that it would placate the old woman. It didn't.

"And who might her kin be? Could be that they're worried about her." Mabel shooed Ethan out of the way to taste the stew.

He watched as she added salt and herbs to the pot and wished he sampled it before she caught him. "Not likely," he said under his breath.

"And why is that?" Mabel had good hearing for someone her age

"Because she claims Nathan Hunter is her grandfather."

Both Mabel and Ethan turned at the sharp intake of breath. Gabriel and Eliza had come down the back stairway and into the kitchen. Eliza stopped in the doorway and glared at her brothers.

"That woman upstairs is kin to Hunter?"

Ethan was grateful for the big ranch

house with the guest rooms on the opposite end from the kitchen.

"That's what he's saying." Gabriel sauntered over to Mabel and peered over her shoulder at the stew. "Actually I heard her say it, too."

"How could you bring her here?"

"Listen, Liza, you liked her right off. You're not going to change your mind and hold this against her." It wasn't a question.

"Oh I'm not? Why is she here then? Why didn't she just go straight to the Double Bar?" Eliza looked ready to battle someone.

Ethan knew the hurt that ran deep within her and would give his life to take away her suffering. "Because she's never met the man. In fact if I guessed, I'd say that she wasn't exactly looking forward to the introduction."

Mabel and Gabriel watched as brother and sister argued. Eliza rarely raised her voice to either brother and when she did, it was usually to Gabriel, who tended to deserve it. Eliza stopped talking, gave her oldest brother a hard look, and took her place at the table.

Mabel served the quiet group and said something about having to bake pies for tomorrow. Ethan knew better—she just didn't want to miss overhearing anything. She knew everything that went on in the family. Even those things everyone thought secret.

Eliza ate, but she didn't appear to notice what she put into her mouth. Ethan contemplated her thoughtful demeanor and left well enough alone. He chanced a look at his brother and immediately wished he hadn't. Gabriel smiled even as he took a bite of Mabel's sweet sourdough roll. Charming one minute, angry the next, and now back to smiling. Ethan just couldn't understand Gabriel half the time. He was grateful that Brenna chose to stay upstairs. He'd rather speak with her alone.

They ate the remainder of the meal with only the sound of Mabel's soft humming to break the silence. Eliza gave her brother another hard look and left the table. Gabriel followed close behind saying something about a poker game in the bunkhouse. Mabel began to sing a soulful and haunting tune. Her voice grew louder and louder until Ethan threw down his napkin and walked from the kitchen. Mabel's loud chuckle followed with another, softer rendition of the song.

Ethan made his way out to the wide front porch and settled against one of the solid dark logs holding up the roof. The sun had set, leaving only a glimmer of the beautiful colors creeping on the other side of the mountains. The crisp and cool air surrounded him as the moon shone brightly in a sky of stars. He thought to settle himself on one of the rocking chairs his mother had set out years ago but was surprised to find one already occupied.

Brenna stopped rocking and remained still and silent when she saw Ethan walk out onto the porch. She had heard the voices carry from the kitchen when she came down the front steps. Brenna had been able to make out her name, but the kitchen was far enough away that she heard nothing else.

After she had cried herself dry for the

second time in the past year, Brenna had put herself back together. Her mother always called crying a "cleansing for the soul." Brenna smiled as she thought back on her parents and then grew cold when she thought of the reasons why she was here. She just wanted some time alone and couldn't bear to stay cooped up in the borrowed room of a stranger.

Brenna had found solace in the rocking chair and looked out over the setting horizon. The sun's final rays of the day slowly kissed the mountains good night and settled in until morning.

She had hoped to be back inside before anyone else ventured out, but here Ethan stood wearing a clean black shirt and black pants with black boots. He still hadn't shaved. The man looked like the devil. She waited for him to go back inside, but instead he turned toward her and his body stilled.

Ethan stood there and looked at the most alluring woman he had ever met. The flame-red hair he admired earlier in town now hung partially down and fell in soft waves over her shoulders. The moonlight reached inward enough to make the red locks glisten. Her face fell mostly in shadow but didn't detract from her beauty. She wore only a shawl over her dress and even sitting down he could see more of her now than he could before.

Brenna grew impatient once again. It didn't matter that she became just as absorbed in watching him as he did her. He was so tall—a large man who appeared to be strong muscle earned by years of hard work. She remembered the stories her father used to tell her of the Highlanders hundreds of years ago. Throwing trees and boulders for competition and running savage through the hills protecting their land. He had made them sound like fierce giants. Ethan Gallagher reminded her of the men from those stories but without the war paint. She didn't think he would need it.

Ethan broke the connection and moved to sit down on the other rocker. He stared into the distance saying nothing for a long time. "Did Mabel see you settled in?"

She nodded, thanking him and then remembered that Mabel said something about a tray of food. She realized she was a little hungry but was reluctant to go back inside.

"I apologize for the reception you received in town. Not everyone in the area is like Bradford James."

"There is no need to apologize. It was . . . unexpected I suppose, but I'm sure every town has their unsavory elements." Brenna pulled her soft woolen shawl of deep gray tightly around her shoulders and set the chair in motion.

"Yes, but that doesn't excuse poor manners."

"Truly, everyone's been kind and an apology is not necessary, Mr. Gallagher."

"Ethan."

"Ethan. Though I can't help but wonder about the reactions from you and your brother when I made mention of my grandfather."

Ethan appeared to think about his answer for a moment before replying. "It was nothing personal, just a reaction."

"I gathered your family doesn't care for him."

"You gathered right." Ethan's smooth voice allured her even when he sounded harsh. "But that doesn't mean our feelings toward you run in the same direction."

"I didn't assume so or you wouldn't have let me into your home." They both quieted for a moment and then she asked, "You didn't mention parents earlier. Do they live nearby?"

A slow smile of remembrance appeared on Ethan's face. "They've passed on some years ago now." Then as though he wanted to relive a pleasant memory, Ethan said, "Every time this year, my parents would head off on a little adventure. All of the paintings you saw on the way upstairs, well those are all of the places they've gone. They always brought something back to remind them of those memories."

"I saw a painting of Scotland."

"That was their last adventure. They told us they'd never seen any place more untamed than Montana Territory until they saw the Highlands of Scotland." They

both sat silent again for a few minutes
longer, each lost in their own thoughts.
Ethan spoke again first.

"I know that you traveled a great
distance to see your grandfather, but you
don't appear to be in a great hurry. I just
wish that you'd consider this a little more
before you ride out to the Double Bar."

Her cool and controlled voice disturbed
even her, and she saw the confused
reaction it brought to Ethan's strong
features. "Your grievances with my
grandfather must be quite serious if you're
warning me away from my own blood."

"The truth is that I like you."

His confession startled her, but she
remained calm and listened. His next
words softened her a little more.

"In fact both Gabriel and Eliza like you.
It doesn't matter that we just met you;
you're already a friend in our minds. We
have some scores to settle with Nathan
Hunter, and I'd rather you didn't get
caught in the middle."

Brenna nodded, slowly stood, and
walked toward the screened door. Before

she opened it, she turned around and in a voice laced with as much disdain as Ethan ever put into his, she said, "I'm grateful for all you've done, but you needn't worry about that, Mr. Gallagher, because I have a few grievances of my own with Nathan Hunter."

5

If Brenna couldn't be home watching the morning mist in Scotland, then watching the sun rise from the front porch of Hawk's Peak ranch was the next best thing. She'd seen few sunrises in her lifetime because more often than not, she woke to mist and rain. Such beauty helped ease the pain of missing home.

The hot cup of strong coffee Mabel handed her when she walked into the kitchen a few moments ago didn't suit Brenna, preferring tea as she did. Though the aroma of the dark brew made her sigh as she watched the steam rise from the cup into the crisp morning air. Brenna sat on the rocking chair and enjoyed the moment.

She forgot her worries for about two

minutes, and then Gabriel sauntered up with a grin and a bright greeting. He settled his large, but lean, frame in the rocking chair his brother occupied the night before.

"The smell of that coffee brought me over this way, but it's certainly your smile that has brightened my morning."

Gabriel grinned at her and before she thought anything of it, Brenna handed him her cup. At his raised brow, she gave a dainty shrug. "I'm not used to such brew."

He thanked her and drank half of the hot liquid. "Are you always such an early riser?"

She looked at him, but his eyes scanned the horizon.

"That I am. My mother and I used to work in our gardens in the early morning hours."

"You don't anymore?"

"No."

Gabriel nodded his head in understanding. "You know I've been meaning to ask, you've got that bit of an

MK MCCLINTOCK

accent, but otherwise your English is perfect. How'd you manage that?"

She smiled softly. "My father hired a tutor from London and my mother was American."

She said nothing more and remained a little distant.

"Gabriel, how did this ranch come by the name Hawk's Peak?"

Gabriel leaned back and stared out at the vast night sky. "Well, our father thought himself an adventurer and that never changed as long as I knew him. He was always running off to some unknown part of the country or so he said. Anyway, he itched to get as far away from city life as he could and then away from the heat of Texas. When he first scouted the northern lands, he rode up to this valley. After weeks of riding and searching, he said he'd never seen anything so beautiful in his life, except our mother of course, but that's another story."

Gabriel grinned and Brenna found herself smiling in response.

"He decided on this spot right off and

knew this piece of land had to be his, so he scouted it a bit more and when he rode up to that ridge up there . . ."

Brenna looked to a small crest slightly to the east of the horizon where Gabriel pointed.

". . . he reached the top and saw nothing but a few trees. That's when he noticed the hawk. He waited as it flew around and around overhead and finally landed at the top of one of the trees. When he went to get a better look, he saw a nest and the hawk not far away standing guard. Being the risk taker that he was, he tried getting up close to see inside the net. The hawk's mate chose that moment to swoop down and protect the nest. Ma said that Pa had some mighty nasty scratches from those talons. He even bore a few scars he showed me later on. He figured that since that hawk lived here first, he ought to let it alone, and he named the ranch in honor of that magnificent creature. To have heard Pa tell it, that same hawk has been living in those trees all these years." Gabriel rocked the chair slightly with his long legs and finished the strong coffee in one swallow.

"That's a lovely story."

"It is that," he said. "But if you want to see lovely, our parents built a small cottage in town near an orchard. It's not used anymore, but it's a nice place to get away."

Brenna gazed out over the land. "I can't imagine getting away more than this."

"It's possible."

Both Gabriel and Brenna turned at the sound of Ethan's voice from the doorway. Brenna hadn't heard him come out onto the porch, but Gabriel didn't appear surprised to see his brother standing there.

"Morning, Ethan."

"Gabriel. Mabel wanted me to let you know that if you plan on eating you'd better wash the smell off from your morning ride."

Gabriel gave a smile to Brenna. "It's been a pleasure, Miss Cameron." He lifted himself out of the chair, slapped his brother on the shoulder, and walked around to the back of the house. Brenna also stood and turned to Ethan when he directed his attention to her.

"Mabel wasn't sure if you wanted to eat downstairs with the family or if you'd prefer a tray brought to your room."

Brenna remembered the food Mabel left in her room the night before. She'd been so hungry but still unsettled that she hadn't eaten a thing.

"If your family doesn't mind, I'd like to eat downstairs."

"Not at all. We're pretty informal around here, so we usually just eat in the kitchen. I'm sure Mabel will set up the dining room now that you'll be joining us."

"She needn't go to the trouble. I don't care much for formalities."

Ethan smiled. "So I've noticed."

Brenna followed Ethan into the house and back to the kitchen. Gabriel now wore a fresh shirt and stood at the wash basin in a small room just off the kitchen. Eliza sat at the table, reading a book on animal husbandry. Ethan offered Brenna a chair and the two men followed suit. For an informal meal, Mabel set a nice table. Brenna's mouth all but watered at the eggs, hotcakes, sausages, ham, and fresh homemade breads that the woman laid out before them.

Once everyone served themselves, they remained silent as the meal commenced. Eliza glanced across the table at her and Brenna wondered if she'd dropped food on her blouse. Gabriel thoroughly enjoyed the meal, and Mabel, who joined them after serving the food, glanced between her and Ethan throughout dinner.

When Brenna ate all she could without overdoing, and everyone else appeared to be finished with their meals, Brenna took a deep breath and asked no one in particular, "Would anyone mind telling me why you hate my grandfather?"

Ever since her conversation with Ethan the previous evening, Brenna wondered what awful things this man did to cause such hatred.

What worried her was the concern in Ethan's voice the night before, and what else she had heard, a warning perhaps? A warning from what? She needed to know and felt she deserved to know. By the looks on all four of the open-mouthed and grim-set faces at the breakfast table, she'd have to say that the Gallaghers didn't agree.

Eliza excused herself from the table. A tic formed in Gabriel's jaw that he tried to soften with a small smile, and Mabel stood to clear dishes. Ethan hadn't moved. Apparently his brother and sister decided they'd leave the telling to the eldest. Either that or Ethan was just slow to move. She was wrong. He stood up and told her to follow him.

When they reached the front porch she thought that they would sit and talk. Then when they walked out to the stable, Brenna began to worry. He won't harm you, you ninny, she thought. But she also hoped that he wasn't going to hitch up the wagon and drag her back to town. Brenna grasped onto the unspoken understanding that she was still a welcome guest. She couldn't pinpoint why, but she did not want to leave the ranch right now.

He surprised her by telling her to wait by

the door and moved to saddle up a couple of horses. One was Ethan's beautiful big black stallion with nary a mark on him and the other, a pretty blond mare, and a good-sized one at that, with a silvery white mane.

With the animals saddled, he motioned her over. Grateful that she wore sturdy boots and a warm shawl, Brenna was caught unawares when Ethan half lifted her frame into the saddle and then mounted his stallion. Her long skirts covered her legs, but the stops of her boots were visible. She didn't imagine there was a side saddle on this ranch.

"What exactly are we doing?" Brenna was unable to keep a little anger from creeping into her soft brogue.

He didn't answer her question right away. "Do you know how to ride?"

"I do."

"Good. Follow me."

Because she couldn't do anything else, and because of the insatiable curiosity, ever a part of her personality, Brenna gathered the reins and followed Ethan out of the stable. Gabriel and Eliza walked toward the paddock as she and Ethan rode passed. Neither looked too happy, but Gabriel once again tried to soften his expression for her with a smile, however grim. Brenna took a deep breath and urged her mount into a gallop to keep up with Ethan.

A short while later, she decided she'd like to kill the man.

"I thought you said you knew how to ride?" He pulled his stallion to a stop near the top of a small crest. They had ridden for about four miles and at a hard gallop for the last two. Brenna could already feel the blisters forming.

"I can. I'm just unaccustomed to this type of saddle. It's rather stiff."

"You'll get used to it." Ethan spoke with confident arrogance and motioned her over beside him and pointed down the hill.

"There it is."

Brenna followed his hand until her gaze fell on a large house in the distance. There stood a barn and a few outbuildings, though not in nearly the scope as Hawk's

Peak. "This is the Double Bar?"

Ethan nodded absently and then finally looked over at her and his stomach clutched. She wasn't looking at him and so he didn't bother to turn away. His first thought was that no woman he'd met compared to how incredibly beautiful she looked in the morning light. He hadn't given her time to grab a hat so the fire-red hair she plaited down her back now flowed free with long curls reaching her shoulders. His second thought was admiration. The woman could indeed ride. Despite her obvious discomfort with the saddle, she kept pace with him and his strong stallion without complaining. Ethan quickly brought his thoughts back to why they'd come.

"Yes, it's the Double Bar."

"Did you not say I should wait?"

"Well it seems that you're not the most patient person I've ever met and since you want answers, I think you should have them."

She still looked confused and said to him, "Couldn't you have just answered the questions at the ranch?"

"I'm not going to answer your questions."

"Then why—?"

"Nathan Hunter's going to answer your questions."

6

Panic quickly settled in. Brenna had planned this ever since her father died. Confront her grandfather, ask him why he sent her mother away, and explain the scandal her father had mentioned. She wasn't ready for the next step.

"Ethan, I can't." She refused to follow him down the slope. He turned back and rode up beside her, his leg brushing up against hers.

"I thought that this is why you came here." Ethan spoke in a calm, soothing voice and behaved as though he possessed all the time in the world.

"It was. To be sure, it is, but I thought to do it in my own time." She watched as that blasted brow of his rose up, but his eyes showed something else—compassion perhaps? Brenna didn't want compassion or sympathy. She just wanted to not be there.

"You didn't think you'd ever get this far, did you?" He wasn't patronizing.

He seemed to understand, which she found she didn't appreciate. "Of course I thought I would get this far, just not this far this soon." Resigned, she looked down the hill to the ranch house below. "I haven't prepared myself and then everything you've said about the man since I've arrived has made me somewhat wary of the man."

Ethan smiled. "I haven't said much of anything about Hunter."

"That I know and there's the problem. It's what you and your family have not said that has me worried."

"But that hasn't changed your mind."

Brenna shook her head. "No. I didn't come all of this way not to face him, but there was something in all of your expressions this morning at the table that had me wondering what he could have done to evoke such hatred in strangers."

"Perhaps our reasons are no different than yours?"

Her head turned quickly to meet his eyes but she said nothing and gave nothing away.

"I won't feel comfortable with you under our roof, at least not with everything between Hunter and my family." Brenna looked concerned and tried to hide it. "You said you had your own grievances with the man and that's your business, but as long as you're at the Peak you're bound to be caught up in the middle of our . . . disagreements. I'd like for you to stay on at the ranch, but I won't feel right about it until you understand what you could be up against."

Brenna listened and sat thoughtfully, her dutiful mare patiently grazing. "Then why not tell me?"

Ethan sighed, somewhat impatiently. "Because it wouldn't be right. Our hate could cloud everything we say and you need to make your own judgments about your grandfather. After, if you decide to stay for a time at the Peak, then at least you'll know the whats and whys."

"That's kind reasoning coming from a man who claims to hate him as much as you do."

Ethan didn't bother remarking on that observation.

She respected Ethan's sense of right and fairness. Brenna didn't travel across an entire ocean, leaving behind everything she knew, without finding her answers. She wouldn't turn scared and run now. With a straight back and determined frame of mind she nodded to Ethan. "All right, I'm ready but . . . "

Ethan waited, saying nothing, though he could see her inner struggle. This woman knew how to survive and if there was ever a quality Ethan respected, it was the will to endure. He knew what she was trying to say, but he wanted her to ask him. He didn't know why, but he needed her to ask.

"I know it's a right I don't have . . . I mean I know you hate my grandfather and you probably never want to see him and you have a lot to do back at your own ranch

. . ."

"Brenna?"

"Yes?"

"What is it?" His whispered question calmed her racing heart.

"Will you go down there with me and be there when I meet him?"

"Yes."

Brenna nodded her thanks, relieved. "Is he going to let you down there?"

"He won't like it, but he will." Saying nothing more, Ethan led the way.

Though not as grand as the Gallaghers, the house appeared well tended. Made entirely of wood except for a couple of stone layers along the base, Nathan Hunter's home looked typical of the ranch houses she saw on the stage ride through the plains. As she and Ethan rode up to the largest of the buildings, a few ranch hands stepped out onto the porch of a small bunkhouse. A few more rode in when they approached. None of them, except one, appeared to have a pleasant disposition. The one who did appeared to be too young to know any better. But it was the meanest looking of the bunch, if not the biggest, who stepped forward. He glared at Ethan and then gave Brenna a mocking perusal. She wanted to hit the offensive man.

"You was the last person I'd expect to see out here, Gallagher," said the grizzled-face, chaw-chewing man.

Brenna visibly cringed; she couldn't help it. She imagined living a hard life had aged him more than his actual years.

"I assure you this isn't where I want to be, Douglas. Is he here?" Ethan looked almost bored. His beautiful horse relaxed a leg and blew out air as though it, too, would rather be someplace else.

"Well now, maybe he is and maybe he ain't." Douglas smiled, showing discolored teeth right before he spit onto the ground.

Another revolting man.

"Well then, why don't you tell him his granddaughter is here to see him?"

Brenna watched the men, and noticed how that comment gained their attention.

"Hunter don't have no kin no more," said Douglas.

"Apparently he does." Ethan said this

impatiently, as though it really didn't matter to him, but he didn't expect arguments about it either.

Brenna grew tired of the older man looking up at them from the ground.

"Then how come we ain't never seen her before?" Douglas said, and pointed to Brenna as though she weren't important enough to speak for herself.

"Perhaps because I've never been to Montana before." The foreign accent surprised the men and some of them gave her a more studied look. Brenna took in a deep breath and tried to ignore them. "I am who Mr. Gallagher says. He kindly offered to show me the way here, and I thank you, sir, to tell my grandfather that I'm here."

Ethan smiled, proud that she had found her gumption.

Douglas still wore his well-used confusion." But you ain't American."

"How astute." Brenna really hoped that she wouldn't have to say anything more, and just when it appeared Ethan wanted to shoot the eyes out of every man there, another much older man walked toward them. Brenna held her breath.

She wasn't sure how, but she recognized, as sure as she knew the blood coursing through her own veins, that this man was her grandfather. It was the eyes. Her mother's eyes, her eyes. She wondered how long it would take him to recognize her. Other than the flame-red hair, the one and only feature from her father, she knew she looked just like her mother did at that age. Ethan moved his stallion closer to the mare, and his leg once again touched hers. She sensed him stiffen as her grandfather walked closer. He really could have been a handsome man if it wasn't for the evil in his eyes. Those weren't her mother's eyes. Her mother never had an evil thought in her life.

"What in the hell are you doing on my land, Gallagher?" The shout reached them before the gray-haired man did. Ethan said and did nothing. He just waited for Nathan Hunter to reach them. When he did, Brenna sent up a silent thank you to her parents for keeping him away.

"I asked you a question."

"He came with me." Brenna kept her voice neutral but was unable to disguise her light brogue without revealing the roiling anxiety welling up inside of her.

His eyes narrowed. "And who are you?"

Ethan intervened. "If we could take this someplace private, Hunter, then questions can be answered."

For a moment Brenna didn't think her grandfather would accept Ethan's suggestion, but finally he motioned his ranch hands away. "Come up to the house then, but make it quick."

They dismounted as Nathan waited on the porch. He refused to let them inside, and Brenna saw how much hatred her grandfather held for at least one Gallagher.

"I don't know what in the hell you think you're doing here or why you brought along your little lady, but you're not welcome here."

Brenna stepped closer to him and her shoulder brushed up against his arm. He could feel her slight tremble, but he knew that Hunter didn't have a clue she was frightened. It pleased him to see that her back was straight and her eyes steady.

"I don't want to be here anymore than you want me here, so we'll get this over with as quickly as possible."

"What over with?"

"I need some answers, and unfortunately you're the only one who can give them."

The feminine voice caused Nathan to turn his gaze downward to look at Brenna. He wasn't quite as tall or big as Ethan and Gabriel, but he still towered over her.

"And who are you, little lady?"

Brenna didn't care for his condescending tone and matched it. "Brenna Cameron, your granddaughter."

Silence filled the air around them on the wooden porch. In the not-too-far distance the sounds of laughing ranch hands and horses could be heard. The sound of shattered glass reached them as though someone had dropped an empty bottle onto the hard-packed ground. They waited.

Brenna didn't have an exact plan, but she didn't doubt that she could pull this off with Ethan beside her. Odd how twenty-four hours ago she'd not even known the man and now she depended upon him. Brenna wanted to finish this chore and ride out of there, never to see Nathan Hunter again.

"My what?"

"I believe she was clear."

"You stay out of this, Gallagher."

Ethan was surprised to see the old man lose his temper. The few times he had spoken with Hunter, he'd been a composed and calculated man.

Nathan Hunter studied her. "I don't have a granddaughter."

"You do. I am the daughter of Rebecca Hunter who married my father, Duncan Cameron. My mother wrote to you after my birth and you sent this in response." Brenna was grateful she put the letter in her pocket that morning. She kept it with her at all times to remind her of why she came here. Nathan grabbed the worn piece of paper and read. The emotions flickering across his face worried Brenna. She wouldn't give him the satisfaction of retreat.

Ethan also saw his reaction and didn't trust Hunter. He took a slight step closer to Brenna until she stood just behind and to the side of him. The distant sound of an eagle carried to them as they waited.

Nathan Hunter crumbled the letter and threw it into one of the spittoons on the porch. "Why are you here?"

"My parents have died."

Her grandfather finally looked surprised.

"My father told me about you before he passed on."

Nathan Hunter's next words cracked her heart.

"I told her I didn't want to see or hear from her again and I certainly didn't want to see you. I got what I wanted, but in the end she managed to turn him, too. So I ask you, what could you possibly want to know that could make you come all the way out here? Let me tell you the only thing you need to know about your whore of a mother. She disgraced her family by running off and bedding down with that Scotsman. Rebecca was to be married that week, but it took her less time than that to give herself to another man and shame her family and her fiancé."

Hunter shouted nearly every word, and Ethan barely resisted pushing Brenna behind him. He guessed she wouldn't stand for that, but the desire to shut this man up continued to grow. Brenna needed to hear this, though, for her own good.

Brenna didn't know what to think or say, but Nathan Hunter obviously wasn't finished with his tirade. She managed to stop him for a moment. "What do you mean? Who did she turn against you?"

Nathan Hunter actually shut up long enough to give Brenna a look of mild bewilderment and gave them both an evil-looking smile.

"I don't know how you couldn't know, though I suppose they wouldn't have wanted to tell you."

"Know what?" Brenna couldn't ignore what he said about her mother and for the first time she could remember, her control dwindled, but she had to know.

"You know, I don't think I'm going to tell you." Her grandfather sneered at her. "Your mother shamed us all when she ran away. I don't owe her daughter anything. You're no better than her, are you? Just arrived and already a Gallagher's whore."

Ethan's right fist wiped the sick smile off of Hunter's face. Brenna was too shocked to do anything but stare down at the old man Ethan just felled with one jaw-cracking hit. She didn't hear the hands running up from the bunkhouse and barn.

Ethan did. He grabbed her by the arm and practically threw her into the saddle and gained his own mount. He looked at her.

"Can you ride?"

Brenna offered him a silent nod, trying for the moment to keep her mind off of what just happened. She finally saw the men running toward them and followed behind Ethan as he raced off of Double Bar land.

Once they gained the hill and were a safe

distance from Hunter's spread, Ethan
stopped his stallion, jumped down, and
pulled Brenna from the mare. He just held
her. He could feel the entire length of her
body shaking.

"I'm so sorry. I shouldn't have taken you
there. I should have just told you what you
wanted to know, but I didn't want you to
think that we clouded the truth. I never
should have let it get so out of hand.
Forgive me."

Ethan's hand rubbed up and down her
back as he apologized and tried to console
her. He blamed himself, and she just
wanted to tell him to stop. The chasm
between her and her grandfather was not
his fault. She knew there had been no love
lost between her mother and grandfather,
but she hadn't realized just how much he
hated his own daughter. *What won't he
tell me? What else had my parents kept
hidden from me?* Brenna didn't want to
leave the comfort of Ethan's arms. Instead
of pulling away, she merely stepped back
enough to look up at him.

"This is going to cause more problems

for you, isn't it? The hitting I mean?"

Ethan just shrugged. "No, it's not. In fact it's something I've wanted to do for a long time."

Brenna leaned back into him, taking solace in his strength.

"I'm sorry."

She silenced him with a finger to his lips. "Don't be sorry. I needed to hear it, I suppose. Only now I'm more confused than before. I won't go back there. My parents were right to keep me away, and now I know why." What hurt the most was what her grandfather said about her mother. Brenna had never known two better people than her parents.

Ethan saw the first hint of tears and pulled her back to his chest. He held her and let her cry as he realized that he never held a crying woman. Not even his sister. Eliza was tougher than anyone ever gave her credit for. Not that he thought she never cried, he'd just never seen it.

When Brenna's tears turned into hiccups, Ethan set her at arm's length and lifted her tear-streaked face up with the back of his finger. He meant to ask if she was all right, but he saw her green eyes bright with tears. The sorrow in them was quickly replaced with confusion and then desire. Ethan wasn't sure if she knew what her eyes told him, but he found it too difficult to ignore.

He found her soft lips one moment, and the next he saw those same lips rosy and swollen, her skin flushed, and her eyes dark with passion. She looked confused. He understood why when she gained her mind. "No one's ever done that to me before." She looked up at him. "Why did you do that?"

"Hell if I know." Well, that wasn't completely true. He wanted to, plain and simple. He didn't answer her question. Unfortunately he said the first thing that came to mind.

"Why aren't you married?" He wished he could take the words back the moment they came out of his mouth. He'd never seen any woman go from passion to anger so quickly.

"That is none of your business, you—"

"Excuse me?"

"Never mind."

Thinking that he couldn't possibly say or do anything to make the situation better, Ethan moved away from her.

"Are you up for riding again?" he asked as though nothing had just happened between them.

She nodded jerkily, and he moved to help her into the saddle since she seemed to have difficulty getting her foot in the stirrup. She pushed his hands away. After a few tries Brenna finally found her seat.

Ethan gained his own mount and set a sedate pace back to Hawk's Peak.

7

"**H**ow'd it go?"

Ethan ignored his brother and went back to the open ledger on his desk. He had taken over the running of the ranch with Gabriel about six years back when their parents had decided that they wanted to travel. Ethan knew his father loved ranching, but he also knew that his father had earned a rest. None of them, though, thought it would be a permanent one. Jacob Gallagher made Hawk's Peak the most successful ranch in three territories, and it was now up to the next generation to keep it going strong. However, at the moment, Ethan found it difficult to record this month's purchases in the column designated. For the past eight hours, Brenna had been the only thing on his mind.

"That well, huh?" Gabriel seemed undaunted by Ethan's dark mood and settled himself in one of the leather chairs in front of the desk. The office looked more like a gentlemen's lounge with a desk in the center of it. Rich leathers and wools, heavy drapes and masculine furnishings, and hundreds of books filled the built-in shelves. Their father always said that if he must suffer through account books, at least he could be comfortable doing it.

"The reason I ask is because I couldn't help but notice the way Brenna looked when I passed her on the stairs earlier."

Ethan didn't look up from the books. "And how did she look?" He sounded suspiciously like he didn't want to care.

"Confused."

Ethan glanced up at his brother. "Confused?"

Gabriel smiled. "Yep. Now at first I thought for sure she'd come back with a face full of tears seeing as how Nathan Hunter is a bastard. Then I thought that perhaps she might be angry rather than tearful. Turns out she just looked confused. Then again perhaps she was a little angry too." Gabriel's twinkling eyes met his brother's. "You don't happen to know anything about that now do you, Ethan?"

"Lay off!"

"Didn't think so."

"Gabriel, so help me . . ."

He decided to give his brother a break. Gabriel couldn't remember ever seeing his staid older brother take to a lady the way he had to Brenna Cameron. In fact, he'd never seen his brother take to a lady at all—well, except Rachel. He knew his brother found companionship when in need of it, but he didn't think it happened that often. The fiery Scottish lass appeared to be doing a good job churning up his brother.

Gabriel turned more serious. "How did it go?"

Ethan set down the pen, no longer able to concentrate, and livid over what happened earlier. Gabriel's goading didn't help. Ethan counted himself lucky that neither he nor Eliza had been at the stable when they rode up.

"Probably about how you're thinking it went." Ethan's frustration focused on his reaction to the confrontation at the Double Bar. He planned to stay away from Hunter until he had proof to bring the marshal with him, and he hadn't been ready for the encounter.

Gabriel nodded and lifted his hands up in front of him in a half shrug.

"So, what now?"

"I haven't the faintest idea." Brenna turned out to be an unexpected, if an otherwise extremely pleasant complication.

Ethan rubbed his hand over his face, realizing that he'd forgotten to shave that morning. "She didn't see the worst of Hunter today, and now that he knows she's here . . . hell, Gabriel, I should have kept her away."

"Does she know about her grandmother?"

"I doubt it. As horrible as the altercation was, I didn't want to add to her pain."

Ethan told his brother exactly what transpired, leaving out the details after they left the Double Bar.

By the time he finished, Gabriel looked just as angry as Ethan felt. "She deserves to know the rest. She'll trust what you tell her now."

"I know that, but I'm not sure how to tell her. When I spoke of Hunter before, I only mentioned a few grievances."

Gabriel raised a brow. "I'd say rustling, rape, and murder are more than grievances."

"We don't have physical proof and besides, Hunter isn't aware that we know about the murder, and we only suspect it was him. The marshal won't touch him until there is hard evidence."

Gabriel sat forward, his midnight-blue eyes turning darker. "Are you telling me that you now don't plan on doing something about this?"

"Hell no, Gabriel. I'd like nothing more than to pull the trigger myself, but unless we want to join him in a cell or a grave, we'd better have proof. Our family has abided by the law all of our lives, and there is no way we're going to change that because some murdering, thieving, bastard is living next door."

Ethan didn't realize he'd been yelling until he sat down and saw his sister at the office door.

"I heard you from the front hall." Eliza's clothes wore dust from a day spent on the range. She looked narrowly at both brothers. "So what's going on here?"

"I agree with Gabriel. She has a right to know the rest of it, Ethan."

Gabriel finished recounting the story to their sister and being a true Gallagher, Eliza never felt the need to keep her opinion to herself.

Ethan found that particular family trait annoying. "Well unless one of you is volunteering to tell her, I'd thank you to keep out of it."

Eliza stood and put a hand on her older brother's shoulder. "I love you, you know that, right?"

He covered her hand with his own. "I

know."

"I've seen something in your eyes in the past twenty-four hours that I haven't seen in a long time. You owe it to yourself to see where it can go." She patted her brother's hand. "And that's all I'm going to say for now." Eliza said goodnight and left the room.

Gabriel turned back to Ethan. "We have another problem."

"Yeah, I know." Ethan swore and pushed away from the desk and glanced at his brother. Since they were as close as kin could be and thought so much alike, they rarely needed to explain themselves to each other. "I know, but I don't know what the hell to do about it."

"Does anyone even know where he is?" Gabriel kept his seat and watched his brother pace. Ethan ran a strong hand through his dark hair and barely kept himself from swearing again. He prided himself on always being the controlled and calm brother, but in the past day, his restraint began to seep away.

"No, but if I chanced a guess I'd say that

Mrs. Hunter just might know."

Ethan stopped pacing, and Gabriel worried at the look on his brother's face. He knew that look. "Let me guess. You're going to look for Mrs. Hunter, is that it? Ethan, I know you and Ma never thought she died, but it's been a lot of years."

"People thought that Ramsey died seven years ago, but we know otherwise now, don't we?"

Gabriel couldn't argue with that.

"Are you going to tell her about him?"

Ethan sat down on the corner of the large desk. "We don't actually know that he's Hunter's grandson. Rumors don't prove anything, and Ramsey never claimed to be anything other than a hired hand."

Gabriel gave his brother a skeptical look. "But you don't believe that, do you?"

Letting out a discouraged sigh, Ethan shook his head. "No, I don't. Not after meeting Brenna. We spent enough time with Ramsey, and I swear they're family."

Gabriel stood to leave Ethan alone with his thoughts, but at the door he turned around. "If you don't plan on telling her soon, I will."

"Stay away from her, Gabriel." Ethan missed Gabriel's thoughtful look when he turned back to the forgotten ledger. For all of the unpleasantness happening around him, Ethan had more on his mind than Nathan Hunter.

"Brenna, may I have a word with you?"

The rocking chair on the Gallagher's front porch had become Brenna's new favorite spot, and she enjoyed stealing a few quiet moments alone. She forgot her worries when she sat there, watching the horizon and listening to the quiet sounds of the wilderness around her. She caught glimpses of who she assumed were ranch hands and imagined what life must be like out here in the West.

Brenna wasn't in the mood to speak with him right now. Propriety and the fact that she slept under his roof dictated otherwise, so she nodded her head and waited for Ethan to sit in the rocker next to hers. He chose instead to lean against the railing directly in front of her, the fading horizon his backdrop.

"I want to tell you a story, but since I don't particularly want to tell it, I'd ask that you don't say anything until I've finished." He waited for her nod of agreement, settled against the railing, crossed his arms, and spoke in a cool, steady voice.

"Over thirty years ago there wasn't much to this place except a trading post and a few dilapidated clapboard houses. My father found this land and went back to Texas to bring my mother up here. They lived here quietly, watching the town slowly build up around the trading post. The land proved to be fertile and the cattle became plentiful. My folks found a peaceful existence on this land with the other settlers who came to Briarwood.

"A man came to these parts and a lot of people lost that peaceful way of life. The area suffered thieving, livestock was found slaughtered or 'accidentally' dead. Most people knew who was responsible, but no one could find proof. The man's wife disappeared. She was well-liked by everyone in the area, including my parents. When she didn't show up for a luncheon with some of the other ladies in town one day, my mother asked my father if he could go out and inquire after her. He did, and when he came back home, he didn't have good news. My father could find no sign of the man, but one of the hands, who'd only been hired on the previous week, let it slip that his boss went out looking for his wife. Everyone on the man's ranch believed her dead and that this man murdered her. That was over fifteen years ago.

"No one ever found the woman or any proof of foul play. Over the years the 'accidents' continued to happen, but nothing could be proven."

Ethan watched Brenna's face for a glimpse of emotion, but she remained passive, waiting for him to finish. He continued. "Years ago, Eliza and a friend of hers, Mary Preston, went out riding toward the north range. Mary's horse got spooked by a snake and she fell off. Eliza got down to help her and didn't notice the riders until it was too late. Eliza tried going for the rifle she kept in her saddle, but one of the men got there first. They recognized her, and they didn't want to have to deal with Gabriel or myself if she came to harm. They held her back and when Eliza wouldn't stop struggling, they knocked her out. But not before she saw the others drag Mary away. A couple of our hands found them little more than an hour later—Eliza still out cold, but Mary had been raped and severely beaten. She died a week later.

"We followed the tracks to the Double Bar. From Eliza's description, we found three of the men who attacked them. Nathan Hunter covered for his men, even when Eliza went back with us and the marshal, but the marshal wanted more proof than Eliza's word. The same week that Mary died, the three men left the territory. When the authorities questioned Hunter, he told them he didn't know who they were talking about. To this day we haven't been able to prove that it was

Hunter's men or that he knew about it."

Ethan stopped speaking. Brenna knew he waited for her to say something, anything. Darkness sneaked upon them, and Brenna noticed the chill in the air, unsuspecting and unwelcome. She looked up at Ethan and wished that she could ride over to the Double Bar and put a bullet in Nathan Hunter's heart. For her mother, for her father, for the grandmother she didn't know who may be alive or not, for Eliza and her dear friend, Mary, who Brenna wished she'd known, and for all of the heartache her grandfather had caused.

"Did anyone ever find my grandmother?"

Ethan slowly shook his head. "I heard a rumor that she ran away up north, but no one saw or heard from her again. A few years after she disappeared, my mother finally received a reply from one of the many telegrams she sent out searching for her. It said that a woman matching the description had ridden through there with a family that summer."

"From where did the telegram come?"

"North of here, a little town called Bright River."

Brenna nodded and stood.

Ethan followed suit. He wanted to pull her into his arms and comfort her as he did before, but his hands remained clenched at his sides.

"Thank you, Ethan."

Confused by her calm reaction, he merely nodded, feeling hopeless as she walked quietly inside through the silent house and up to her borrowed room. Ethan continued to stare at the door, lost in his own thoughts. Mabel walked up from the other side of the house.

"I like her."

He nodded.

"She's stronger than you might think. No one comes as far as she has on her own without strength."

He nodded again.

"Ethan?"

He finally turned to look at Mabel.

"It's not my place to tell you what to do with your life."

Ethan gave her a look that clearly said;

When haven't you told us what to do with our lives?

She ignored it. "I will tell you this. In all of two days, you've met, brought home, and made yourself champion over that young lady. In two days her life has been turned upside down. She's living with strangers in a world she doesn't know, and she's learned the unfortunate truth about her family. Through it all, she's shown more strength than any woman should have to in her situation."

"And?"

"You're a fool, Ethan Gallagher, if I have to say anything else." With that, Mabel walked inside and let the screened door close softly behind her on its oiled hinges.

Ethan gazed through the quiet night. He could barely hear the sounds of laughter from the bunkhouse. He knew Gabriel would be there winning yet another week's earnings off the hands. One might think they'd learn by now not to play with him. Ethan smiled to himself.

This land wasn't just a place they hung their hats. More than wood and stone taking up space on the dirt, this land represented their parents' legacy, and God willing, that of many generations after he was gone and buried. Blood, sweat, and endurance built Hawk's Peak and he'd be damned if he'd allow Hunter to cause any more hurt and pain. The man took up too much space on this earth.

The empty look in Brenna's eyes had unsettled him, but he knew he couldn't fix the situation. She needed to work through it on her own. Mabel was right about one thing, well everything actually if one bothered to ask her. Ethan Gallagher was a fool. This woman, this incredibly strong and amazing woman found her way into his life, and he kept mucking things up at every turn. Ethan desperately wanted to make things right because that's what he did—fixed things. Powerless to heal her pain, he knew he'd spend every breath he had trying. Yes, Ethan was a fool—an absolute fool in love.

8

Eliza tended to sleep the nights through, but she credited that to being so tired at the end of each day from all of the energy she expended. Gabriel slept like the dead. It took noise similar to dynamite going off under him to wake him up, unless, of course, the sound seemed suspicious, at which point he'd be up like a flash. Ethan, on the other hand, rarely slept deeply. He hated it, but learned to live with it. Even with a glass of brandy before bed, he still slept half awake. So it wasn't a great surprise when he heard the soft footsteps in the hallway before the quiet knock at his bedroom door.

Stark naked and comfortable, he didn't relish getting dressed. He knew it wasn't Gabriel with footfalls that light. He couldn't think of any reason for Eliza to wake him up at three o'clock in the morning. That left only Brenna, and she wouldn't be knocking at his bedroom door. Annoyed at the disturbance and wondering what his sister wanted, Ethan got out of bed and yanked on his pants even as another quiet knock sounded. He didn't bother buttoning his pants all the way and padded barefoot to the door, yanking it open.

"Eliza, what do you . . ." Ethan stared in surprise at Brenna barefoot and standing at his bedroom door.

Brenna couldn't stop looking at his bare chest. Brenna's thoughts wandered back to the kiss he gave her. Had it really only been the previous morning? she wondered and forced her eyes up to his face.

"Sorry to bother you. Now that I think on it, this can wait until you're up for the day. I couldn't sleep and wanted to ask now, but really this can wait."

"Brenna." He couldn't help but smile as he noticed how her eyes kept wandering downward, and she kept forcing them back to his face. She looked pretty when she got flustered.

"Why don't you just ask me whatever it is that sent you to my door in the middle of the night?"

"I need you to tell me how to get to Bright River."

That's not what he expected. "I hope you're asking out of simple curiosity."

"I need to know if my grandmother is still alive. I've been thinking about this all night, and I have to know."

Ethan noticed how she wrung her hands within the folds of her skirts. Brenna had removed her shoes but hadn't bothered to change out of her dress. He wondered if she slept at all that night.

"Bright River is less than half the size of Briarwood and a long ride from here."

"Is it too difficult?"

He wanted to say yes but couldn't lie to her. "No, physically you could make it, but it's too dangerous. There are a lot of hunters and trappers roaming the hills between here and there, not to mention the Indians who are unpredictable in these parts." Ethan hoped to dissuade her, but he knew by the determined look in her eyes that he failed.

"Please. I could ask in town, but I don't know who to trust."

Well isn't that just my luck. "You're going no matter what I say, aren't you?"

"Yes, I am. I have to." She stopped wringing her hands. Her eyes remained steady and fixed directly on his.

How in the hell did I get into this? he thought. "We'll leave tomorrow." He moved to shut the door, but she stopped it with her foot.

"What do you mean 'we'?" She actually sounded nervous.

He found that oddly satisfying. "I mean that if you want to go, you're going to have to put up with me going with you."

"That's highly improper."

"If I told you how to get there, chance is you'd get lost and if you didn't get lost, you'd probably be attacked by some wandering miner or misfit and left for dead. Now, if you want to go, I'm going with you. Take it or leave it."

He really thought she would say leave it,
or at least take a little time to think about
it. She surprised him once again.

"I'll take it." She smiled and turned back
down the hall quickly tiptoeing back to her
own room.

Ethan shut his door none too gently,
pulled his pants off, and got back into bed.
Two minutes later he swore out loud,
pulled his pants back on along with his
boots, and headed for the cold swimming
hole just north of the stable.

Before the sun rose, Ethan waited with the
horses in front of the house. He
questioned his good judgment many times
since he had volunteered to take Brenna
up north in search of a grandmother she
never met and wasn't sure if she even
lived. His sister also questioned his
decision, but Ethan didn't have the
answers.

Gabriel hadn't been surprised.

"You think that I'm out of my mind,
don't you?" he asked his sister.

"No, I'm just wondering why you didn't

lock her in the bedroom until she found some common sense." Eliza stared at him with eyes like his own, full of worry, just as his would have been if it was her leaving alone with a stranger. "Just be careful. There's a lot more going on here than her search for a lost relative."

Ethan nodded. "I know." Ethan hugged his sister and turned to Gabriel who stood against the porch railing with a somber expression.

"For all her worries about a chaperone at the ranch, Brenna sure didn't have a problem going on this wild chase alone with you."

Ethan stared out over the land rather than at his brother. "She's desperate to find the truth, no matter who the company is."

"Oh, I think it matters." Gabriel slapped his brother on the back. "Just take care."

Ethan knew his brother didn't just worry about his physical well-being. He worried about Brenna. Ethan's patience to get on the road wore thin. The sun barely peeked over the horizon, and he wanted to get started, but Brenna didn't seem to be in a hurry. Just when he considered going in after her, Brenna stepped out onto the porch followed closely by Mabel.

Ethan stared. *How in the hell is this going to work?* His sister had loaned her a pair of riding breeches, thinking that they would be more comfortable for the long ride. Since Brenna was shorter and curvier than Eliza, Brenna also borrowed a jacket that went down far enough to preserve her modesty. The breeches clung enough to cause Ethan worry as they did nothing to hide her form. She wore her hair plaited down her back and a wide-brimmed riding hat that he assumed belonged to her since he'd never seen it before.

Brenna carried a satchel in one hand that she handed to Gabriel when he offered to tie it on the pack horse. Normally Ethan wouldn't have bothered with the extra animal, but he couldn't be sure how long the trip would take, and they had at least three days before they reached Bright River. Nothing but wilderness stood between them and their destination.

"Now I've packed you plenty of food for today and lots of jerky and dried fruits. The rest you'll have to cook as you go along." Mabel hovered over Brenna, doing her best to talk her into staying put, but Brenna would have none of it. She hugged the housekeeper with whom she'd become fast friends, and thanked Eliza for the borrowed clothes. The finer riding outfits she'd brought from Scotland suited Cameron Manor far more than Montana.

Ethan gained his mount as Gabriel moved to help Brenna with hers, but she agilely lifted herself into the saddle. The breeches proved to be most useful.

"You don't have to do this." Ethan looked directly at her.

"Yes, I do."

Everyone said their good-byes and with a nod indicating that she was ready, Brenna followed Ethan away from Hawk's Peak.

Ethan set a mild pace the first day, but she attributed that to the pack horse they brought along. Brenna felt anxious to reach Bright River, but Ethan told her they had a few days ride ahead of them. She hoped Ethan might enjoy some good conversation to help pass the time. He proved to be stubbornly quiet. Ethan answered her questions with a few one-word answers, and she finally gave up and turned her attention to the scenery.

The beautiful country spanned around them, and Brenna wondered if she could settle in Montana for good, watching the sun rise over the mountains and the cattle grazing in the pasture while she curled up next to a handsome cowboy. On one hand the thought nearly broke her heart. To leave Scotland permanently—she wasn't ready to think about that. She might however consider staying if someone gave her a good reason.

The first day seemed to drag on interminably. They stopped only once to water the horses and eat some of the jerky and dried fruit Mabel had packed. Brenna groaned with relief when Ethan announced they were finally making camp for the night. She'd been an avid rider in Scotland, but hours in a stiff saddle didn't help. When they stopped, she slowly eased out of her saddle and excused herself to find some privacy.

Ethan watched her walk into the trees knowing she'd be safe as long as she stayed within shouting distance. The thick junipers and blackberry bushes provided good cover among the trees. He once again questioned his sanity by bringing her out here and decided that he was still a fool, plain and simple, because a sane man would never have done it. He kept his distance during the day, deflecting her attempts at conversation. Ethan felt like a cad for doing so, but maintaining distance was the only way he could remain a gentleman on this ride.

When she returned, Ethan had already unsaddled the horses and started a fire. "The weather won't turn tonight, but if you'd like the tent up, I can take care of that for you. It gets near freezing this time of year."

Brenna had been surprised to discover

that Ethan even packed a tent for her, but she didn't want to use one that night. She had never enjoyed the novelty of sleeping out of doors, regardless of the cold. Even when she had traveled through the Highlands with her parents, they found accommodations all but one evening, when they brought a spacious tent with all of the trappings of an upscale hotel room.

"I'm fine without it. I'll just keep my bedroll close to the fire."

Ethan shrugged as though he didn't care one way or the other and pulled a bedroll and extra blanket from the pile of items unloaded from the pack horse. He handed the items to her without saying a word, and Brenna accepted just as quietly.

The silence might have been uncomfortable if Brenna wasn't so tired. Sounds of the night carried to her in the quiet. The distant howl of a wolf and the night call of a nearby owl felt oddly comforting. She didn't know if it was weariness or because Ethan stayed near to keep her safe.

Ethan sneaked glances in her direction

as he set up his own bedroll and heated some beans to go with the cold chicken Mabel had sent along. He didn't pay too much attention to what Brenna did until she started pulling one item after another out of her satchel. He saw a small mirror, a silver brush, a silver jar holding who knew what, a washcloth, a brown glass jar with some kind of liquid in it, a bar of soap, and a nightgown.

"What on earth are you planning to do with all of that?" He stood up and walked over to her bedroll until he loomed above, casting a shadow over her.

Brenna didn't even bother to look up as she proceeded to put everything back into the satchel.

"I just wanted to be sure I had everything. I'm going to the stream for a bath."

She sounded serious, but he didn't believe her.

"Is there a problem with that?"

"Aside from the fact that it's close to freezing up here and you'll probably end up half frozen from the water, or the fact that there's a variety of critters crawling, slithering, and walking around out there, and not to mention that you'd have to strip down to nothing in order to bathe properly and put on that frilly white thing, so yes I'd say there's a problem with that." He hadn't quite yelled, but something close to it crept into his voice.

Brenna, however, remained undaunted. She tilted her head slightly to the right and smiled, knowing full well she was about to irritate him further, though she had no idea why she wanted to. "Well, I used to swim in the rivers and lochs in Scotland, and I assure you that the frigid temperatures of those make your little streams feel like you're swimming in a tropical current. Though I don't like crawling, slithering, and walking things I can't see any more than the next person, I'm not about to let them scare me away from my bath, and I had absolutely no intention of stripping down to nothing as some of my garments are also in need of washing. As for my nightgown, I have no intention of sleeping in trail-worn clothes only to wake up smelling rank."

With a bright half smirk and a nod of her head, Brenna walked away from the camp down to the stream hidden by some wild blackberry bushes.

He'd never seen anyone jump back from upset so quickly.

Ethan didn't know if he wanted to go after her and drag her back to camp for a good lashing or go down to the stream and join her. Since neither would bring about gentlemanly results, he opted for a small smile as he watched her leave. This woman showed him so many different sides of her in three days that he found himself wondering which one could be the real Brenna Cameron.

He was surprised at his own envy of her. She found something good, something to hope for, even after the encounter with her grandfather. After all that she learned, she found reason to not give up.

Brenna waited until she stood at the water's edge, exasperated with the man, but grateful he insisted on joining her.

Since she'd been bored in the saddle throughout the day, she had memorized different landmarks. She didn't doubt that if she tried to find her way back, she'd still get lost.

She carefully set her satchel down on a rough rock next to the water and stripped down to her camisole and bloomers. Neither garment was the most practical thing to wear under the borrowed breeches, but she refused to do without them. Testing the water with a quick dip of her foot, she determined that she exaggerated. It didn't feel like a tropical current, but it certainly wasn't as cold as some of the rivers back home. Brenna submerged herself into the water as best she could and washed with her heather-scented soap she had made in large batches back home. Once she was adequately clean from hair to feet, she moved to the bank, only she didn't make it out of the water.

Ethan heard the scream and bolted to the water. He arrived at the water with his gun drawn, ready to protect her, but when his eyes rested on Brenna he couldn't see anything wrong with her. He moved closer and saw her face. He'd never seen eyes so big in his life. He followed her terrified gaze until his eyes settled on the retreating rear end of a small black bear.

Ethan wanted to laugh and it took all of his control not to.

Brenna finally found her voice. "What took you so long? That thing could have attacked."

Now he did laugh. He just couldn't help it. "I take it you've never seen a bear before, Miss Cameron."

"A bear? No I haven't actually seen a bear before, *Mr. Gallagher*, and I'll thank you to stop laughing at me."

"Your scream was enough to scare it away. It just wanted to find a light meal." He pointed to the blackberry bush she chose to bathe near.

"I'll have you know that I've seen far worse creatures in my lifetime than a measly bear. Just startled me is all."

"Uh-huh."

Brenna scowled at him, and he stopped

laughing only when he noticed her state of undress. The delicate white undergarments clung to every curve, and her long red hair rioted in wet curls around her shoulders and arms. The bright moon overhead left nothing unnoticed. She was still submerged to her knees and appeared to be turning blue. Ethan cleared his throat and turned away, giving her his back.

"You'd better get out of there before you turn sick."

Feeling too foolish and cold to care about anything else other than a hot meal and blazing fire, Brenna quickly left the stream and removed her wet clothes to put on her nightgown. Ethan had been right about that necessity. She gathered her satchel, but couldn't stop her teeth from chattering. "I'm ready."

He turned around and thought she looked like the most adorable creature he ever laid eyes upon. For all of her bragging and gumption, she was obviously cold and her nightgown clung to a few patches of wet skin. He held out his hand to her without saying a word. She offered him a grateful smile and took it.

Once Brenna settled on her bedroll, she immediately brushed and dried her hair by the fire while Ethan started another pot of beans. The first one had burned when he ran to fight off her ferocious attacker.

Brenna plaited her hair while still damp and thanked Ethan when he handed her a plate of food. They ate in silence, and when she was about to turn in for the night, he spoke.

"The next time you want to bathe, let me know and I'll be happy to stand guard for you." He didn't even try to hide his grin.

Brenna wanted to throttle him.

The next two days progressed just as the first, with the exception of bathing. She soon discovered that Ethan had been serious about keeping guard. She would heat a pot of warm water over the fire and clean as best she could with her washcloth.

On the fourth day of riding, Brenna's back and legs ached every time she moved, though she refused to say anything. She found relief late that afternoon when they spotted civilization in the distance—a town with actual people.

Ethan noticed that Brenna shifted in the saddle, likely from soreness, and he admired the fact that not once did she complain. As they came upon Bright River, he saw the first smile he'd seen from her in three days.

They led their horses down the dusty road through the center of what could loosely be called a town. Ethan directed them to the front of the trading post and dismounted while she took in what there was of Bright River.

Brenna really didn't think "town" was the right word, but it did have the trading post, a telegraph office, and houses scattered up and down the dirt street. A questionable boarding house with a sign out front that said "Miss Annie's" stood across the street from a tiny saloon.

Brenna eased off her mare and resisted the urge to groan when her feet hit the ground. Her eyes found Ethan, who stood and spoke with a tall thin man sporting a trim gray beard. Brenna guessed him to be the owner of the trading post. Ethan motioned her forward and she answered with a scowl.

Brenna ignored the indecent looks sent her way by some of the locals gawking from the few buildings, Brenna walked up the steps to where Ethan and the other man stood. Ethan gave her a once over as though making sure she didn't sustain any injury between the horse and the porch and introduced her to the owner of the trading post.

"This is Elias Lawson. Mr. Lawson, this is Miss Brenna Cameron."

Mr. Lawson tipped his hat. Ethan took her elbow, the first physical contact he voluntarily had made in over two days, and nodded toward Elias. "Mr. Lawson is the one who sent the reply telegram to my mother about your grandmother."

Brenna's interest in the man escalated and she gave him her full attention.

"It's a pleasure to meet you, Miss Cameron." Elias gave her a quick look from head to toe.

Brenna ignored the fact that she looked

like filth after their time on the trail. "It is a pleasure to meet you as well, Mr. Lawson."

Elias grinned. "A Scottish lass if I'm not mistaken."

"Yes, sir."

"I knew me a Scottish lass once before. Well at least she claimed to be Scottish, but I can't right be certain."

He appeared to be deep in thought over this when Brenna asked, "Mr. Lawson, if you did in fact see my grandmother, I wonder if you might spare a few moments of your time?"

"Well now I'd be happy to."

Ethan interrupted them both before Brenna could speak again. "Why don't we talk over supper, Mr. Lawson?" Ethan squeezed her elbow as if to tell her to keep quiet and be patient.

It annoyed her to do so, but she nodded her head in agreement.

"That'd be just fine. You know I think I met a Gallagher once. Went by the name of Jacob."

"My father."

"Good man, I recall. Met him down Texas way," he added for Brenna's benefit.

She merely nodded.

"That must have been some time ago. Now if you'll excuse us, we need to find lodging for the night."

Elias held out a hand to stop them both from moving away. "Now I wouldn't be going and trusting any accommodations you might find around here. Not a hotel or decent boarding house in town, but I do have a couple of extra rooms upstairs and a place where you can wash up. There's a lady that comes in once a week to clean so the linens are fresh."

Ethan considered this a moment and looked at Brenna. Even dirty and worn out from the ride, she still looked beautiful. She also looked tired, and he didn't have the heart to make her sleep outside another night.

"We'd appreciate that, thank you." He felt her relax beside him.

"You go ahead and bring what you need upstairs, and we'll talk later over a hot meal," said the store owner.

Brenna nodded her thanks to Elias and didn't argue when Ethan grabbed her satchel from the pack horse, refusing to let her carry it. She followed him to the second level of the trading post and down the hall to two small rooms. She saw the bed and it brought her a small measure of joy. Ethan set her satchel down on the faded quilt and informed her that he saw the washroom next door to the bedroom. She thanked him, not noticing when he stopped for a moment in her doorway before leaving and closing it behind him.

Brenna gathered what she needed for her toilette and went to the room next door. She was surprised to find such a room in the primitive setting of Bright River, but the room had a large copper bathtub next to a small wood stove. On the stove sat a large pot of water, and when she tested the temperature, she found it to be only room temperature but enough to suit her present needs. Mr. Lawson couldn't have been expecting guests. A few more buckets of tepid water sat next to the tub and she used those with the large pot to fill the tub.

It wasn't grand, but it was a bath and a better one than the cold stream offered a few nights back. Unfortunately, the water cooled quickly and she hurried to finish up. Once she washed her hair and scrubbed the last of the trail dirt off, she finished dressing in her only clean clothes, a warm wool dress of simple lines in a deep green. She brushed and plaited her hair, not wanting to take the time to dry it. A soft knock at the door stilled her motions and she waited.

"Brenna?"

She opened the door. Ethan apparently found somewhere else to clean up because his hair looked clean and damp, curling a little around the collar of his black chambray shirt. He shaved for the first time since Brenna had met him. He possessed an exceptionally fine face but she thought it better to ignore that.

"I just wanted to know if you'd like to eat now or wait until you've rested. There isn't a decent place to eat in town, but Elias has made up a nice meal if you're hungry."

In answer, her stomach growled and she couldn't help but smile.

"I'd say eat now, rest later," he replied with a grin.

"Yes, I could eat something. I just need to ask Mr. Lawson what to do about the tub."

Ethan looked around her, then walked into the small washroom. He studied the tub for a moment, pulled up his sleeve, reached into the water, and pulled out a small plug in the side of the tub. The water moved through a makeshift pipe through a small hole in the wall and down the side of the building. "We had a similar set up at the ranch before my father modernized a bit."

"I did wonder how you managed to have indoor plumbing so far away from a city."

Ethan shrugged. "My mother convinced my father that if she was going to live on the ranch, he'd better give her indoor plumbing. At least as much as he could for being in the middle of Montana." He grinned. "Ma usually got what she wanted."

"Well, I'll just put my things away and meet you downstairs."

He made no move to leave. "I'll wait."

Brenna shrugged as he had done and put her toiletries back in her satchel and placed her soiled clothes on a wooden chair in the corner. She'd have to ask Mr. Lawson if someone in town could wash them for her, though she might be better off waiting. The town appeared to be lacking in amenities.

Ethan waited in the hall for her, his shoulder and hip pressed up against the door frame. When she came out of the bedroom, he frowned at her. She wasn't sure what to make of that and decided to ignore him. They went downstairs to Mr. Lawson's living quarters. Ethan pulled out a chair for her at a table already set with simple metal tableware. Elias came in from the front of the store and smiled in greeting.

"Well now, you must be feeling better." Elias didn't wait for a reply but shooed Ethan away, and told him to take a seat. Brenna continued to ignore Ethan but it was growing more difficult. Focusing on ignoring him only made her more aware of his constant presence. That and she didn't know anyone else there, and though she would be loath to admit it to him, she rather depended upon him for her safety. Ethan followed her example and ignored her right back.

Elias brought a large iron skillet over with beef steaks along with a bowl of corn, thick slices of brown bread, and a jug of spring water.

Thinking that someone else must have done the cooking, she asked if they needed to wait for anyone.

Elias laughed. "Nope, afraid it's just me around here. As for the cookin', well, my dear departed wife made me stand in that kitchen every blessed time she cooked and wouldn't let me leave until I learned how. She said it wasn't fair that she do all of it. I spent so much time in that kitchen that I finally gave in."

Surely he exaggerates, Brenna thought, but she smiled at the older man and offered to serve. He nodded his thanks.

Once everyone had their meals in front of them, Brenna couldn't wait any longer.

"Mr. Lawson, if you would be agreeable to it, I'd like to know about my grandmother. You said that you met her as she passed through here?"

Mr. Lawson took a long drink from his mug, glanced at Ethan whose gaze focused on Brenna, and turned his attention to her.

"Well, I can't say we met exactly, just more like a quick hello and she left. I remember her clearly, though. Prettiest lady I'd seen since my wife passed on. Couldn't figure why she'd travel with that tattered family, as well-mannered and dressed as she was. She seemed to be in a hurry and most folks who come through here like to keep to themselves, so I didn't ask."

Brenna tried not to let her disappointment show. "You responded to the telegram from Mrs. Gallagher, though."

"Yes, I did. Jeb Dickson, the telegraph and postal operator, brought it on over here to me. You see, just about everyone who comes through Bright River stops in here. So when he showed me the telegram, I said that I'd seen her."

"She didn't happen to say anything at all? Perhaps where she planned to go?"

Elias thought a moment and shook his head. "Nope, she didn't say anything like that. Like I said, she seemed to be in a hurry."

Brenna's frustration quickly grew. "Did you happen to notice in which direction she traveled?"

"As a matter of fact I did. I remember standing out front talking with old Jeb about his horse that came down with colic a few days before. He had to put the poor thing down in the end. Never did see a case of colic that bad, and Jeb really loved that horse."

Brenna fought the urge to tell Mr. Lawson to hurry.

"Now let's see. Jeb and me faced north, then we turned when that rickety wagon left town and they headed west."

"Are you sure they went west?"

Elias thought a moment and then nodded. "Yep, it was west because I remember Widow Perkins come out onto her front porch to beat a few rugs, and her house is to the west of the store." He nodded as though agreeing with himself. "Yep, they went west."

"West could be a lot of places, Brenna." Ethan finally spoke. He noticed the excited look in her eyes, but most of this land remained wild and untamed. There was no telling where her grandmother went off to or if she even survived.

Brenna chanced a look at Ethan, the first since they sat down for their meal. She knew he wasn't deliberately trying to be cruel. After all, he did bring her this far, but at the moment she didn't want to hear defeat. Brenna needed hope.

"Isn't there any town west of here? Any place at all?" The desperation in her voice made Ethan relent, just a little.

"There's a small settlement a bit west of here called Desperate Creek, but there's not much there except a few farms."

Elias nodded his agreement. "I went out

there once myself some years back, just for a look. They don't have a blessed thing out that way except, of course, those small farms. A few of them come back this way once or twice a year for supplies, but that's about it."

Ethan watched Brenna as she worked something out. She smiled, catching both Ethan and Elias off guard. A person just didn't see many smiles like that.

"Mr. Lawson, I thank you kindly for your hospitality, but I won't need that room for tonight after all." Elias wasn't sure what to say to that. He nodded and stood when she did. Brenna missed the worried look he shot toward Ethan. Brenna offered him another dazzling smile and went upstairs to collect her things. Ethan caught her as she packed up her satchel with her dirty clothes.

"What in the hell do you think you're doing?"

Eliza ignored his outburst. "You really shouldn't curse."

Ethan looked incredulous. "I will curse whenever I bloody well please. Now what are you doing?"

With satchel in hand, she ignored him and went for the door.

He blocked it. She thought for about a second that she could move him, but the man was just too big and too strong. She stood and faced him.

Ethan would have enjoyed the fire and determination in her eyes had the situation not been serious.

"I'm leaving, Mr. Gallagher, now if you'll excuse me I'd like to get a few hours in the saddle before complete darkness sets in.

"You thought to just leave and go riding out to Desperate Creek on your own, didn't you? For the life of me I can't figure out why you think I'd let you."

Brenna definitely saw the anger in him churning now.

"Mr. Gallagher—"

"Ethan."

"Ethan. Regardless of what you may think, I believe I could make it just fine on my own to this Desperate Creek settlement. I have no intention of staying here tonight when I could be a good distance there before dark."

Brenna really didn't want to go alone. In fact she doubted she could get halfway there without getting lost. She'd always been resourceful, but this wilderness could devour her. But she needed to get out to the settlement, whether she went alone or not. She knew Ethan didn't want to come this far, let alone add extra days to the journey. Brenna wanted to give him an out, but he wasn't cooperating.

"You're not going."

"In fact I am."

Ethan sighed and ran a hand through his clean, tousled hair. "Why didn't you ask me to go with you?" he asked softly.

Surprised, Brenna didn't think before answering. "I didn't think you wanted to come. I was giving you a way out."

"A way out?"

She nodded.

Ethan stepped inside the room and closed the door behind him. He reached out and grabbed her satchel. Too surprised to react, Brenna let the bag go. He moved toward her as she backed up.

Ethan wasn't going to have that, so he reached out and pulled her to him. He leaned down to nuzzle her neck and when his mouth hovered just a breath away from her ear and Brenna turned weak in his arms, he whispered in a harsh tone.

"Next time you want to give me a way out and go off to get yourself killed, thinking that I won't care, remember this." He turned his head and crushed his mouth onto hers, pulling her up against him. Losing the battle before it began, Brenna reached her arms around his neck and held on. He ravaged her lips, drawing her mouth open, telling her without words what she did to him and what he wanted to do to her.

Brenna didn't know what was going on inside of her, but she never wanted it to stop. She faltered and became limp in his arms, and if Ethan's hold on her hadn't been so tight, she might have fallen. If he wanted to take her on the bed, she wouldn't argue.

Ethan stopped abruptly and pulled away, holding her up only until she regained her composure. Brenna looked up at him in question as he let her go completely.

"It's too dangerous for the horses to leave right now. Be ready to leave at first light."

9

Brenna couldn't decide which would be a better death for Ethan Gallagher. A knife wound through his black heart or a bullet through his calculating and twisted mind. She really didn't want him dead, but if he came close she could live with it. If she stopped lying to herself, Brenna might realize that she didn't want him injured at all. She just wanted him writhing in agony and preferably by her hand. Why he thought she'd enjoy two hours of breakneck speed on the back of her horse, she couldn't fathom. Not only did he bark at her when she arrived one minute later than the ten he allotted, he practically threw her onto the saddle, tied her satchel to the back of her mare, got on the back of his own horse, and left the town and the pack horse behind. She spared a glance at his stallion and saw that he at least transferred some of the provisions.

Once outside of Bright River, Ethan spurred his stallion forward and the race began. They didn't rest until they reached a small creek bed almost two hours later.

The animals showed amazing endurance but desperately needed a rest. Brenna wished that she could have shown the same. She dismounted and grabbed the saddle for support. She wasn't about to let Ethan see her in this condition. The hateful man probably wouldn't even notice. Brenna avoided looking at him as she unhooked her bag and walked slowly to the creek.

Ethan wanted to swear—a lot—and at no one but himself. He unsaddled the horses, grateful that they had been bred and trained for stamina but wishing that he'd stopped sooner for them. Ethan brushed them both down with a rag he wetted with cool water from the creek and set them to graze for the evening.

Blame for his present condition rested entirely on him. He was angry with himself for being unable to control his feelings toward Brenna and took it out on her and the horses. Ethan honestly couldn't decide which of the two he felt sorrier for.

They should have turned back for the ranch. He doubted that they would find anything at Desperate Creek. What little he remembered about it painted a dirty picture consisting of some ramshackle farm houses, a few planted fields, and some outbuildings. Ethan remembered Elizabeth Hunter well and knew no other lady as fine except his own mother. He couldn't imagine her throwing her life away to such dire circumstances, even to get away from Nathan Hunter. But again, he knew Nathan Hunter.

His thoughts turned back to Brenna. She endured better than he thought she could. He really should have known.

Ethan smiled. He didn't miss the fire in her eyes on numerous occasions and wondered what might happen if that spark ignited. He thought he'd like to see her lose control. He kept to the fire until he realized that she'd been down by the water too long. Ethan listened but didn't hear a thing coming from the creek. A tremor of fear coursed through him. He mocked her when she saw the little black bear, but he should have stopped in his laughing long enough to warn her that dangers really did exist out here, including bears.

Ethan raced down to the water and stopped cold. Lying down on a bed of autumn grass with her torso leaning against a large flat rock, Brenna slept. He was in awe of her beauty. Brenna had stripped down to her chemise and must have washed herself, because he couldn't see a speck of dirt on her ivory skin. Ethan walked softly up to her and smiled. It's a wonder she wasn't half frozen. He leaned down next to her resting form and gently lifted her into his arms. Her curvy frame fit perfectly as she settled her cheek against his shoulder. Ethan carried her back to the warmth of the fire and laid her out on his bedroll. He unrolled her blanket and covered her with it. After gathering her things by the water, he returned to find her still in deep sleep. Betting that she'd stay asleep until morning, Ethan went back to the creek to wash himself off. He changed into a clean shirt and pants, set his jacket and boots with the rest of the tack, and spread his long body out on the bedroll next to her.

In her sleep, she curled up against him seeking warmth. Ethan felt her chilled skin and pulled her even closer, wrapping an arm and leg around her to ward off the cold.

He was in deep trouble. Ethan knew it from the moment he stopped her descent into the street back in Briarwood. At that moment Ethan made a decision, though a part of him still tried to figure out what that decision meant. He may still be unsure as to why everything happened the way it did, but he was definitely sure about one thing. Could he have a life with someone who loved him? With that question in his thoughts, Ethan fell asleep holding her in his arms.

"Oooh!" Brenna groaned and rubbed her posterior. Her pride had prevented her from asking Ethan to slow down yesterday. Brenna tried wiping the morning haze from her eyes as she pushed the blanket back from her face, but the sudden movement made her pause. She immediately brought it up around her shoulders. The early autumn air felt bitter, feeling much like a cold bath on a cloudy day, and she wore only her thin chemise. Brenna tried thinking back to the night before.

She remembered walking down to the creek with her satchel, planning to wash up and change into her nightclothes, but she couldn't recall anything beyond the washing. Brenna had to admit that nearly a year passed since she had slept so well. She glanced around her and wondered where Ethan took himself off to. His horse was tethered nearby with her mare, so she didn't worry he left her. The man surely wouldn't leave behind his stallion, she thought. The scent of coffee wafted from a tin kettle over the fire and her stomach grumbled. Brenna added not having the energy to eat the previous evening to Ethan's ever growing list of sins.

She debated leaving the warmth of the bedroll, but Ethan sauntered back into camp holding a wrapped cloth and smiling.

"Good, you're awake. I found some berries. Not much around here this time of year, but it'll tide us over, and I'll fry up a few hotcakes." He set the berries on a log next to the fire, grabbed her bag from where he set it the night before, and dropped it on the ground next to her. "You'll probably need that." Ethan went back to the task of preparing breakfast and a sudden thought occurred to her.

"Why have you never asked me to cook?"

"Can you?"

"I can't, but you didn't know that."

"True. Then again, despite the fact that you've wanted to see my neck stretched for the better of four days or that you shoot daggers at me with those emerald-green eyes, I figure you for the type of person who'd offer if you could. Since you didn't offer, I didn't ask."

Brenna had no response to that, so she wrapped the top bedroll around her, picked up her things, and walked down to the creek bed.

Ethan smiled at her retreating back. Sometime between sleep last night and this morning, he'd decided to stop acting like a jerk and a fool, and he felt much better about this little side trip to Desperate Creek. It was taking longer than he expected but the ranch was in good hands with Gabriel and Liza. Being in such close proximity with Brenna alone all of the time frustrated him but that didn't matter. Ethan smiled again remembering her look of confusion. He behaved civilly to her and she just couldn't figure out why. Well, let her go on wondering, he thought. And as soon as he figured it out, he just might consider explaining it to her.

Not long after she left, Brenna returned in a semi-clean, semi-wrinkled dress. He knew she didn't have a chance to wash the breeches his sister loaned her. *Thank God for small favors.*

Brenna walked cautiously back into camp and set her things near the mare's saddle. She glanced at Ethan as she picked up and shook out both bedrolls. Looking at Ethan and back to the rolled up blankets, a frantic thought took over.

"Where did you sleep last night?"

"On my bedroll."

Oh dear. "But there are only two and both covered me when I woke up."

He looked at her and nodded. "True."

She really wanted to throw that pot of coffee at him.

"Where did you sleep last night?" This time she sounded panicked, and Ethan couldn't let her think what she likely thought.

"Nothing happened." He paused in his cooking and looked at her. "You fell asleep by the creek, I brought you back here. It was cold and I thought you could use the extra warmth. I'm not so noble as to sleep directly on the damp ground, so I *slept* next to you."

Red with embarrassment, Brenna

nodded and carried the bedding to the tack pile and returned to sit on the log next to the fire.

Ethan handed her a metal plate with a few hotcakes, some jam, and the few berries he managed to find. He fixed his own plate and began eating until he realized that she wasn't.

"I know it's not Mabel's cooking, but you haven't complained so far."

Ethan watched her closely as she struggled with some inner worry. Her next words surprised them both.

"Thank you, for last night I mean," Brenna said and feeling flustered she continued. "I'm grateful you were close—I felt safe."

Ethan merely nodded, though he really wanted to ask her about the last time she felt safe.

Brenna turned her attention to her food. With her hunger appeased, she offered to clean the plates. When she once again returned from the creek bed, the horses were saddled, their gear tied on back, and the camp cleared.

"We still have a bit of a ride ahead of us, so we'd better leave."

"I thought it not far from Bright River. Surely we covered a good distance last night." She had the sore muscles to prove it. Perhaps Elias's "bit of a ways" was farther than hers.

"We did, but we can't run the horses like that over this mountain. It will be rocky in some places with patches of snow and ice, so we'll have to take it slowly." Ethan handed her the reins to the mare and mounted.

"How could a wagon have made it up here?" She climbed into her own saddle.

"There's another way around the mountain. It takes a few extra days, but it's the only way unless you go up and over." He nudged the stallion forward with a slight touch of his knees.

"Why didn't we go that way?" Brenna pulled up alongside Ethan. "I mean if this way is more dangerous."

"Not dangerous for us, just for a wagon." Without further explanation, Ethan and his stallion began the climb up the steep mountain trail. Brenna didn't think the ride so bad until they came to a rocky slope that appeared better suited to mountain goats. Brenna had difficulty getting the mare to keep moving forward. After a few tries, the stubborn animal finally climbed upward.

Midday approached when they reached the start of the downward trail. Ethan glanced over his shoulder at Brenna, about to explain the ride down when he saw the flash of fear cross her face. She leaned slightly over the side of her mare and looked down. Her face turned green.

Good God, she's afraid of heights. The top of a mountain was not the place to learn such things about his riding companion. Ethan needed to distract her and fast, and he knew only one way to do that. "Tell me about your parents."

Ethan might expect her irritated glance if he had asked her to strip down and ride down the mountain naked, but he assumed her parents would be a pleasant topic. He understood as well as anyone what it meant to lose your mother and father to tragic circumstances, but speaking of them always helped him feel closer to their memories.

"What do you want to know?"

Ethan brushed his horse up against her mare and guided the animal toward the steep mountain trail. Brenna stiffened in the saddle beside him, but didn't pull back on the reins. "Tell me your favorite memory of them."

She smiled, and Ethan took advantage. He knew the mare would follow his stallion.

"There's a tall hill not far from Cameron Manor with a cave tucked inside a cropping of rocks. My father discovered it when he was a child, and when I was old enough to ride on my own, he took me up the hill to explore the cave. One summer afternoon, I begged my parents to take me up there for a picnic. I found the most beautiful stone that day, and gave it to my mother. My father had the stone set in a pendant, and she wore it every day."

"What happened to it?"

"It was lost when my mother fell from

her horse."

Ethan stopped once they hit the end of the trail and waited for her horse to step up beside his. "I'm sorry, Brenna. I didn't mean for the memory to sadden you."

"It doesn't, not as I thought it would. My memories of them hold more joy than sadness." She looked behind them at the mountainside. "Thank you."

Something stirred inside of Brenna when Ethan stared at her, and she couldn't help but wonder when this strange shift had taken place between them.

Ethan released his gaze and faced forward in his saddle, the spell between them broken . "It'll be an easier ride now."

He kept a sedate pace as they rode across the land, leaving Brenna to her wandering thoughts. A light breeze lifted the flap of her jacket back, but she let it go. The cool air felt good against her body. Ethan handed her some dried beef when they stopped to water the horses.

The sun lay low in the sky when they reached Desperate Creek. Brenna expected something entirely different, and glancing at Ethan, she could see that he held a similar state of surprise.

"I thought you and Mr. Lawson said this settlement consisted of nothing more than a few ramshackle farms."

"We did." He turned in his saddle looking around at the mountains just to make sure they arrived in the right place.

"This is Desperate Creek, is it not?"

Ethan nodded in confirmation to her question. "This is the right place. Come on."

Brenna rode alongside Ethan toward a pretty, two-storied, white farm house. Someone planted a well-established garden off to one side, though the plants showed a recent cutting. On the other side, a small fence enclosed a yard with a straight wooden swing hanging from a tall apple tree. Brenna could picture the spring blossoms and the tree bearing fruit. Off in the distance stood a scatter of small box houses, all in good repair, some white, others just board. Quite a few acres of well-tended farm land and a couple of corrals with horses and a milking cow finished off the picture. Chickens clucked in their pens and hogs scrounged around in a slop bucket.

"This place doesn't look so desperate, Ethan."

"No it doesn't. This doesn't make sense either." They rode their mounts up to the largest of the houses, and he told her to stay put for a minute. When she balked he softened the order.

"I just want to make sure it's safe for you to get down."

"It certainly looks safe enough."

That's what bothered him. "Please."

Since the man never once said "please" to her, she agreed and remained on her horse.

Ethan climbed the few steps to the front porch just as an attractive older woman with graying hair opened the door and stepped out to greet them. Brenna saw that she was wearing a dress of good quality, though a bit outdated, and had a long apron tied around her waist. She also looked about ready to faint.

Ethan nearly fell over in surprise. He

dropped his hat when the woman took him into her arms. No small feat for such a petite lady.

Brenna sat there in surprise as Ethan and this woman hugged each other. When they pulled away, she saw that they both smiled. Brenna couldn't however, hear what they said.

Ethan couldn't believe they found her. "We thought you died."

"I know, and I'm so sorry for that." The woman wiped a few stray tears from her eyes. "How on earth did you find me?"

"I didn't think we would."

"We?"

Ethan nodded and told the woman not to disappear as he went back to the horses for Brenna. He lifted her off of the mare and the smile on his face told her something good happened.

"What's going on?" He placed a finger to her lips.

"I'd say a miracle. Come on." Ethan took her hand and pulled her along to the porch. He practically set her right in front of the older woman, never letting go of her hand.

"Elizabeth Hunter, I'd like you to meet your granddaughter."

10

Tears fell unbidden down Brenna's cheeks, but she didn't bother to wipe them away, her surprise and joy too overwhelming. Her grandmother hugged her so tightly she had no other choice than to take every breath she could lest she expire on the spot.

Elizabeth Hunter finally stepped back and held Brenna at arm's length. They stood about the same height, but where Brenna possessed curves and strength, Elizabeth was straight and soft. Elizabeth remained a handsome woman who wore the years of her life with great pride. Her eyes sparkled the way they do when one knows they are blessed with a good life. It was a beautiful face with a kind smile barely causing creases around the eyes.

Brenna saw a bit of her mother in the woman before her, and an overwhelming feeling of comfort washed over her. The women studied each other, taking in every detail they could.

With tears in her eyes, Elizabeth finally spoke. "You're Brenna, aren't you?"

Brenna tried to recall if Ethan said her name, but she was certain he hadn't.

"How did you know?"

A deep sadness fleetingly crossed the older woman's face and just as quickly shook it away. "The two of you had best come inside. There is much to say."

Ethan thought to give them some time alone and started for the horses, but Brenna took his hand. He saw the plea in her eyes and smiled at the trust they promised.

He leaned close. "The horses need tending. I'll be right back, I promise." He squeezed her hand and she nodded, and followed her grandmother inside.

Ethan unsaddled, watered, and released the horses to graze before Elizabeth finished pouring tea. He left their tack and gear on the edge of the porch and found the ladies in the front parlor. Ethan took a moment to look around, and what he saw impressed him. Elizabeth ran away from her husband and found herself a new life, a good life from the looks of things. *Hunter would be furious if he knew how close his wife hid*, he thought.

Ethan studied the two women as he walked into the feminine room, their resemblance unmistakable. Both possessed high cheekbones and the same alabaster skin and stubborn chin. Brenna sat on a settee across from her grandmother and glanced about the room. Neither spoke. Elizabeth motioned him in, and he took the seat next to Brenna. Ethan filled the remaining space, found her hand, and gave a gentle squeeze of comfort. Elizabeth finally broke the silence.

"I never truly imagined that this day would ever come. When Rebecca left so many years ago, I resigned myself to believing I'd never see her again or ever know my grandchildren." Elizabeth pulled a small white handkerchief from her skirt pocket and blotted her eyes. "I wish this could simply be a joyous occasion, but I wouldn't feel right with myself if I did not clear the past."

Elizabeth's sad countenance was apparent. "I should perhaps begin this story back when your mother, my Rebecca, still lived at home with us in Texas."

Brenna saw how difficult this was for Elizabeth and offered her an encouraging smile. "Please, tell me."

"Rebecca was set to be married one week before she met your father. I didn't care for the match, but her father arranged it and Rebecca reluctantly agreed, believing she had a duty to her family—to her father. I knew she wasn't happy with the decision, but her father somehow managed to convince her. The man she planned to marry came from the wealthiest family in the area, and Nathan was determined to join our families and our ranches.

"Then Rebecca met your father, Duncan.

A young and handsome man, touring the country and enjoying his manhood—until he met your mother. They loved each other from the first moment, and I couldn't have been happier for them. The problem, of course, remained that she was set to be married. She told her father that she wouldn't go through with the wedding. Nathan threatened to disown her immediately, but Rebecca didn't care, nor did Duncan. He loved her and didn't care about her money. Duncan hated your grandfather for the way he treated Rebecca. They left the day before the scheduled nuptials and married once they left the territory.

"I received a few letters from her before her father found out and began to have all mail held until he picked it up at the post office. If there had been other letters after that, they didn't reach me. The last letter that your mother sent arrived soon after your birth. Nathan found all of the letters and burned the whole stack.

"We eventually moved up here and the time finally came when I could stay with him no longer. I ran away. I couldn't tell anyone where I had gone to, not even your mother, Ethan. It broke my heart not to say good-bye."

Ethan offered her a small nod of understanding and let her continue. Brenna still listened intently, her features not betraying what she felt. This was the second time she heard the word grandchildren—plural—and it bothered her greatly.

"I went north and made my way through Bright River with a young, poor family. I had money of my own from before I married Nathan and never spent it, so I decided to start a new life. When we came farther west to Desperate Creek, I knew this place could offer me safety and comfort. It was little more than a shanty village at the time. The young couple decided to stay on with me, and I sent the young man back to town for supplies. Eventually with the help of the few young families already here, we turned this little place into a self-supporting farm."

Elizabeth stopped speaking and picked

up her lukewarm tea. She took a tentative sip as if she needed to do something with her hands.

Brenna's first words would shock her grandmother, and she wished there could be an easier way to say it, but it needed to be said. "They've passed away."

Tears filled Elizabeth's eyes. "When did it happen?"

"Mother died almost seven years ago from a riding accident. Papa passed on from pneumonia earlier this year."

Her grandmother didn't have a chance for that to sink in when Brenna added, "I've met him as well."

Elizabeth seemed to know who "him" meant. "I wish I could have saved you from that meeting."

Brenna nodded in understanding, and her own eyes misted.

"Why did you try to find me? Most everyone already believed that I died. Why come all this way?"

"I have no other family, and I wanted to find out why my grandfather hated my mother so much." Brenna told her about the letters she found.

Elizabeth looked uncomfortable. So did Ethan for that matter. Brenna's eyes glanced back and forth between them, as she wondered what other secret had been hidden from her.

"There's more, isn't there?"

Elizabeth nodded.

"I had hoped that your parents might have told you, but I suppose they had their reasons." Elizabeth shifted in her chair. "You have a brother, Brenna. A twin."

The world spun rapidly around her and everything Brenna knew, everything she believed and treasured in her life no longer mattered. Her world dropped out from under her. She was livid enough not to trust herself to speak. Hurt, confused, and uncertain if she could forgive her parents who could no longer defend their actions. Either Elizabeth didn't speak the truth, which Brenna doubted, or her parents lied to her, which made the betrayal unbearable.

"Brenna?" Ethan held her hand in his lap and rubbed her knuckles with his palm.

She finally found her voice. "How is that possible?" Brenna felt weak. "How could I have a twin brother and not know?"

Her grandmother moved to kneel beside the sofa, a lithe woman for her age. "I am so sorry. Your parents probably thought they had time enough to tell you."

Brenna nearly yelled. "I'm twenty-five years old. How much time did they need?"

Elizabeth retook her seat across from them as both she and Ethan waited for Brenna to calm down.

Brenna's trembling voice betrayed the hurt and anger she felt. "What's his name?"

Ethan answered her. "Ramsey."

She swung her head around to face him. "You knew."

"Only the rumors, but no, I wasn't certain. It was a long time ago."

She gave him a look that said she'd deal with him later. "Why did I never know about him? My twin would have been born in Scotland."

Elizabeth answered this time. "Your grandfather, being an evil man, threatened your parents. When he found the letters about your birth and realized that there was a grandson, he demanded that he be sent to Texas. He felt it his right to rear the next generation and claimed that your parents stole his grandchild, his male grandchild. Ridiculous, of course, but that is how he saw things. Rebecca and Duncan refused many times, but Nathan threatened my life and swore he would do whatever it took to get them to comply. I didn't know until it was too late. One year after you were born, they gave in. Nathan nearly followed through, and your mother made a choice. To lose her own mother forever or her son for a time. A nurse traveled all the way to Scotland to pick up the child and bring him back."

Ethan remained silent throughout the exchange, and he could see the inner struggles that Brenna dealt with. He wanted to take all of her fears and worries away. To take the past year of sorrows from her life.

"What happened to him?"

"I wish I knew, Brenna. He kept in

contact with me after I left. He was the only one who knew where I'd gone. Ramsey hated living with Nathan, but I know he stayed for me. I stopped hearing from him about three years after I'd left the Double Bar."

Brenna turned to Ethan with bright eyes. He knew what those eyes asked of him but he didn't have the right answers. "I don't know where he is. I'm sorry."

Brenna nodded solemnly and stood up. "If you would both please excuse me." She left the house but neither one of them followed after her.

"Mrs. Hunter . . ."

"Please call me Elizabeth. I haven't been Mrs. Hunter for many years."

"My mother would have my hide, but all right, Elizabeth," he added with a half-smile. "Do you plan on remaining in Desperate Creek?"

Elizabeth looked around her. "This is my home now. By law I'm still married to Nathan Hunter and if I went back . . ." A chill coursed through her. "I shudder to think what that man might do."

Ethan understood and actually thought it for the best considering all that transpired over the years. They lived in different worlds now, and she created a safe haven here.

Almost two hours later, Brenna returned to the sitting room where Ethan and Elizabeth remained in quiet conversation about his own parents. Ethan could tell that she'd been crying and though her eyes looked dry, he noticed a definite brightness to them. She appeared calm now, more in control, and almost accepting of what she had been told.

Brenna finally went to kneel in front of her grandmother. She took the life-worn hands of the older woman into her own and looked up at the loving face she regretted not knowing all these years. "I don't understand why they kept all of this from me, especially the knowledge of a brother. I know it will take a long time for me to come to peace with what my parents did."

She bowed her head slightly, still unable to believe. "They betrayed not only me, but my brother as well, and I'm not sure how to handle that. I don't blame you for going away or hiding here. I've met Nathan Hunter, and I wouldn't wish that life on anyone. Perhaps, you'd allow me to come visit on occasion? I would like to know you better."

"You're not staying?"

"No, I'll be returning to Briarwood for a time until I figure out what I'm going to do with my life. Ever since Papa died I've been searching for answers. Now that I have more than I bargained for, I need some time to sort things out."

"You're going to look for your brother, aren't you?" her grandmother asked.

Brenna nodded. "I have to. He deserves to know about me just as much as I did him."

Elizabeth patted her granddaughter's hands. "I understand, and please come visit as often as you can."

"I'll bring her back any time she wants."

Elizabeth thanked Ethan, but Brenna only offered him an odd look. He held her gaze for a moment until Elizabeth drew their attention back.

"I hope that you'll at least stay for a day or two. There's so much I'd like to share with you, Brenna."

Ethan agreed to stay for a couple of nights and went back out to the porch to bring in their belongings. Elizabeth told them that the young family she came here with all those years ago lived in the next house over. The woman took care of washing clothes for everyone in the settlement. Brenna and Ethan both gave their thanks at the offer. When the woman, a petite woman named Molly Carson, came by to pick up their garments, she told them they'd be ready the next day.

Brenna and her grandmother spent the following two days close to each other, though Ethan couldn't help but notice the faraway anxious looks that appeared in Brenna's eyes. In just the short time they'd known each other, he learned much about her. Ethan knew that she was impatient to go searching for her brother. Lost grandparents were one thing, and Brenna could always take joy in finding her grandmother. A twin brother you never knew about was something else. Twins possessed a bond closer in blood than the one they shared with their own parents. Ethan understood the power of family. He loved his more than life and would do anything for them. Ethan also understood love enough to know that he would do all that he could in order to help Brenna find her brother.

Ethan spent the whole of the two days walking through the fields to see what Elizabeth and the other settlers managed to do with the once desolate landscape. He spent the rest of the time listening in and offering a few stories of his own about his family. Ethan learned a great deal more about Brenna in that time. Her eyes filled with love when she spoke of her parents, and he knew that she loved them still, but try as she might, the feeling of betrayal still lurked and she clung to it.

When it came time for them to leave, tears threatened to flow from their eyes. The two women became close in such a short time, and Brenna promised a return visit.

Elizabeth pulled something out of her pocket and handed it to Brenna. "This belonged to your mother. I know she'd want you to have it."

Brenna looked down at the beautiful locket in her hand, made of pure silver with a picture of her mother and father on the inside. Tears misted Brenna's eyes. Her anger could be set aside for just this moment.

"How did you get this?"

"Your father commissioned someone to take the picture after he met your mother. He gave her the locket as a gift, but in their haste, left it behind. I should have sent it to her, but I wanted something of Rebecca close to me."

Brenna hugged her grandmother and whispered a soft "Thank you."

Ethan had the horses ready and helped Brenna into the saddle.

"I'll bring her back soon. I promise."

"Thank you, and thank you for watching out for her."

Ethan smiled at the older woman and

asked Brenna if she could ride. She nodded and they rode away from Desperate Creek. More tears never fell from her eyes because Brenna knew her grandmother lived and that she would see her again. Brenna was more determined than ever to fill the remaining voids in her life.

They stopped off in Bright River for supplies and the pack horse, then made the four-day journey back in a record two and half days. She sensed how much Ethan wanted to return home.

When Hawk's Peak came into view, Brenna's heart warmed at the sight. She had only spent a couple of days at the ranch, but in that time, it became as much her home as Scotland.

Gabriel did his best to stay astride a wild, bucking horse, and Eliza sat on the corral fence, watching and occasionally yelling something to her brother. She noticed the two riders first and jumped down from the fence, letting out a loud unladylike whistle to Gabriel.

The mustang he worked decided about that time to admit defeat. Gabriel walked the animal in a few circles and turned to see what caught Eliza's attention. Seeing his brother, Gabriel jumped down from the mustang and handed him off to one of the hands, instructing him to lead the animal around for a bit.

Gabriel met up with his sister near the stable and waited for the riders to approach. With a big smile, Gabriel walked up to Ethan and slapped his back. "It's good to have you home, brother."

"It's good to be home."

Eliza rolled her eyes. "You weren't gone that long." She took the reins on Brenna's mare as Gabriel helped Brenna from the saddle. Brenna looked trail worn and dirty, but something about her had been transformed.

"Your trip was successful?" asked Eliza

"More than you could imagine. We'll tell everyone all about it as soon as Brenna and I have a chance to clean up, eat some of Mabel's cooking, and sleep."

Gabriel removed Brenna's satchel from

the saddle. Eliza and Ethan handed the reins to an unfamiliar, skinny young boy who chose that moment to come out of the barn. Ethan raised his eyebrows in question.

"Carl's nephew's visiting for a few days," said Gabriel, and left it at that.

Ethan let it go as he preferred to focus on Brenna. She looked as though she wanted to topple over. He nudged his brother aside and gave her his support. The action wasn't lost on his siblings.

Eliza's gaze passed between her older brother and Brenna. "There's a new reverend in town by the name of Thomason. He came out to the ranch yesterday to introduce himself."

Ethan gave his sister a curious look. "That's fine but why are you telling me this?"

Brenna caught on quicker than Ethan. "There's no need for a priest. Nothing happened, I assure you." Brenna pulled away from Ethan. "Nothing happened."

Ethan didn't say anything, and Eliza just shrugged. Gabriel stood back and grinned at the entire exchange. He excused himself to go clean up, and Eliza said she wanted to check on one of the breeding mares.

Ethan tried to help Brenna into the house, but she moved away.

Ethan sighed. "Don't let what Eliza said upset you. In her own twisted way, she complimented you."

Brenna looked at him like he was daft. "Since when is believing someone is a loose woman a compliment?"

"She didn't mean it that way."

"Then what pray tell—"

He answered her unfinished question. "She likes you, and it was her way of saying she'd have no objection to you being in the family."

Brenna truly didn't have a better response than, "Oh."

Ethan, however, didn't appear bothered, and Brenna let the subject drop.

Ethan opened the door and followed her inside. They could hear Mabel's cheerful singing from the back of the house. They both went upstairs and walked down their respective hallways, Brenna's well-traveled bag firmly in hand. Ethan's eyes followed her as she walked down to her borrowed room and closed the door.

Frustrated now more than ever, Ethan found his own room and nearly slammed the door closed. He had been bothered by what Eliza said. His biggest problem at the moment seemed to be that he experienced a complete turnaround. He went from not caring about women except when necessity called for it, to finding himself fallen in love with a contradictory red-headed Scot.

Oh yes, I love her. Ethan was a big enough man to admit it, but he didn't have a clue what to do about it. Brenna was just now finding some balance in her life since her father's death, and he knew he didn't have the right to lay this confession on her shoulders.

He'd keep quiet, but he didn't like it. Ethan did know that when his sister mentioned the new reverend, he had seriously considered dragging Brenna to the church and worry about the consequences later.

Ethan ran a hand through his dirty hair, which reminded him that he desperately needed a bath.

11

Brenna sent out a silent thank you to Mabel when Carl's nephew lugged in a large copper bathtub.

"Tommy Hanson, Miss Brenna." The young boy smiled. "Miss Mabel thought you might like a bath in your room instead of downstairs."

"That was kind of Mabel, but did you bring this upstairs?"

"No, Miss Brenna. There's an old bathing room down the hall. I'll be right back with the water."

Tommy left Brenna alone, but it wasn't long before he returned as promised. After three trips up the stairs carrying buckets of steaming water, Brenna's guilt outweighed her desire for a full bath."

"I won't need any more water, Tommy.

Thank you."

Tommy looked at the tub and then at his empty buckets. "But it's not full, Miss Brenna."

"It's perfect. Thank you for your hard work, and please thank Mabel."

The boy blushed, nodded, and left the room.

Brenna ached in places she didn't know existed, but the hot water soon worked the stiffness out of her sore muscles. Once she washed her hair and removed the trail dirt from her body, Brenna left the tub, wrapped her thick, warm, dressing robe around her body, and sat in a cushioned chair by the window. She made quick work of using a brush to dry her long tresses until the thick curls shined. Only a slight dampness remained as she pulled the mass back with a thin blue ribbon.

Grateful to be back in the possession of her trunks, Brenna rustled through and found a blue silk dress she'd not worn since coming west. Too weary to dress quickly, Brenna laid the dress on the bed and slipped into her chemise. Thinking to just lay down for a moment, she crawled into the middle of the large poster bed and pulled the top quilt over the lower half of her body.

Ethan went downstairs hoping to catch Brenna before dinner but couldn't find her anywhere on the lower level. He grew impatient. The others gathered in the formal dining room, and Mabel shrugged off the oddity and smiled. Ethan excused himself for a moment without offering an explanation. He hesitated when he reached her door. It took him a moment before he knocked softly. After a few more knocks and no answer, Ethan opened the door a crack to blackness, except for the soft light casting shadows near the bed. Ethan might have worried if he didn't feel her presence in the room. It was a feeling he felt comfortable with, knowing she was close.

The thick carpets running along the wood floors muffling Ethan's footfalls. He walked to the foot of the bed and stopped, leaning against one of the posts. *My beautiful angel sleeps* This was the second time he came upon her in such a state, and he found himself wanting to comfort and protect her even more than before. Brenna seemed so vulnerable when she slept, and he knew she slept like the dead.

Not wanting anyone to come upon them, for Brenna's sake, he gently pulled the soft quilt up and around her smooth white shoulders, blew out the low lamp, and left the room just as soundlessly as he entered.

Brenna woke to muted light creeping through the curtains covering the expanse of windows. It took her a moment to remember she rested back at Hawk's Peak, tucked away safely in the guest room. The events of the past two weeks rushed back, bringing her to a sitting position. *Had it really only been so short a time?* She let it all sink in and in the end recognized a new feeling settling in her heart—hope. She mourned her father's passing and would always miss him. She found a new sense of family with her grandmother, and even though her grandfather turned out to be a severe disappointment, she finally had answers to questions from her parents' past. *I could have a future here, but is that what I want?*

She vowed to find her brother if it took all her energies. She clung to the hope that he still lived and readied for the day.

Brenna found the house quiet and with a quick look at the large clock on the landing, she realized she'd slept through most of the morning. She was famished and went to the kitchen to beg a light repast from Mabel. She collided with Ethan as they both came around a corner. He reached out to steady her and didn't remove his hands right away.

He grinned. "Glad to see you're awake."

She smiled back to cover up a soft blush. "I didn't realize I was so tired last night. I'm just on my way to see Mabel."

"She'll be happy for the company. She harassed me last night for keeping you away so long. Said the place didn't feel the same without you."

Brenna felt confused. "I stayed here for only a couple of days before we left."

Ethan shrugged. "It seems that's all it took." He released his hands from her arms as though he just realized he held her. Ethan turned to leave when she called his name.

"Yes?"

Brenna chided herself for feeling nervous around him. "I want to thank you for the time you took to help me to find my grandmother. It must have been difficult to stay away from the ranch for so long."

"It was no problem."

Brenna hesitated, then stared up at him, her green eyes bright and hopeful. "With everything you and your family have already done, I don't want to be more of a bother."

"What is it?"

"Would it be possible to get a ride into town?"

He visibly relaxed. "Sure, Gabriel and I planned on going in for supplies in the morning. Eliza has a few things she wants us to pick up for her as well."

"I'll make sure I'm packed."

Ethan stopped her this time with a

strong hand on her shoulder. "What do you mean packed?"

"To go into town." Brenna was confused at his change in attitude.

"You mean for good? Not just a day trip?" Ethan's eyes turned dark and Brenna edged slightly away.

"I thought you understood. If it's a problem, then I can wait and hire someone to come out for my trunks later." Brenna tried to keep from stammering, but she failed.

Ethan removed his hand from her shoulder and stepped away. "No problem."

His voice sounded suspiciously angry, but his face made her think he didn't care one way or the other.

"We'll be leaving at sun up." Without another look her way, he walked out the front door.

Her hunger appeased, Brenna left the house in search of something to keep her mind off of her earlier conversation with Ethan. No matter how hard she tried to prevent it, a heaviness filled her heart. She found Gabriel in the stable, brushing down his sable gelding and answered his charming grin with a smile of her own.

"Well it's good to see your pretty face today." He held out a brush to her in question, and she automatically took it and went to the other side of the gelding.

"It's too beautiful a day to stay cooped up indoors and heaven knows I've spent enough time in bed."

"You earned it from what I heard." Gabriel moved around to the front of the animal so that he could look at her.

"Oh, and what did you hear?"

"Just that you had a hard ride with few comforts. I'm impressed a foreigner managed to make it through as well as you did, and I know you impressed Ethan."

"Humph." Brenna made no other sound and continued brushing down the legs of the strong animal.

Gabriel looked down at the top of her head and mulled over his thoughts. He recalled the conversation he had with Ethan the night before. It had been pleasant enough up until Gabriel asked his brother how things went with Brenna. Taking it the wrong way, which he never did in regard to women, Ethan told Gabriel to mind his own business. That ended the conversation.

Even if nothing did happen, which Gabriel believed since he doubted Ethan would dishonor her in that way, something did happen out there between his brother and Brenna.

"This guy here is done in for the day. We enjoyed a long ride this morning, but if you'd like I can saddle up a couple of the other horses."

Brenna grimaced and cast a sideways smile at Gabriel. "If I sit another horse right now, I'm liable not to move properly for days. I'd better stick to my own two feet for a few days."

"How about a walk?" He took the brush from her and set it alongside his on the tack table.

"I'd like that."

They left the stable and walked out into the warm sunshine. Only a few clouds marred the azure sky. Gabriel showed her a spot near one of the large ponds where she could stand and watch the geese that made their home there every year. She watched a slight ripple in the water form from the stream bringing in the water. Another outlet on the other side released the water into another stream. It was an idyllic setting, and Brenna imagined a sturdy house right on the other side of the water in the grassy clearing. Fruit trees and pine surrounded the house, and in her dreams, she held the hands of a tall, dark-haired man. It was a fanciful imagining, but she held onto it just the same.

When they finally made their way back to the house, Brenna laughed at something Gabriel said and didn't notice Ethan standing on the porch. Gabriel did and immediately sobered. When Brenna finally noticed Ethan, her heart's pace picked up and she offered a soft greeting. Ethan stared hard at his younger brother and Gabriel gave it right back. He stepped just a bit closer to Brenna as if to protect her.

"Nothing for you to worry over, Ethan."

"I wouldn't dream it." His eyes finally moved away and touched on something in the distance. Gabriel swore under his breath, and semi-confident that his brother wouldn't make a jackass out of himself, he told Brenna he had to see to a few things before the evening meal.

Brenna watched Gabriel walk away, but the tension she felt between the two brothers still simmered in the air.

"Is everything all right, Ethan?" she ventured to ask.

"Yes. Are you sure you're up for leaving tomorrow?" At the flicker of emotion in her eyes he added, "I mean if you aren't still too tired from the trip north."

Brenna hid her disappointment with a sinking heart. She supposed it was too much to hope for. Her fanciful dreams always did take her a little far. Her father encouraged them though, even at her mother's disapproval. "A bright imagination keeps a girl interesting," her father used to say.

Brenna cleared her throat of the sudden

lump that formed. Do I really expect him to ask me to stay? she thought. She still needed to find her brother and that would be easier to do from Hawk's Peak. She thought she hid her disappointment well. "Yes, I'll be fine to leave in the morning."

Ethan flicked the piece of straw he'd been chewing onto the ground. "Good." His footsteps echoed as he followed the porch around the side of the house, leaving a shattered heart in the silence.

The rest of the afternoon and early evening dragged on for Brenna. She found little comfort in the book borrowed from the Gallagher's library and soon found herself back out at the pond gazing across to the clearing.

When the first hints of darkness caressed the big open sky, she reluctantly went back to the house. The family gathered casually in the relaxed sitting room. Ethan stood at the sideboard watching his siblings compete in a chess game. She noticed that Ethan poured himself a healthy portion of brandy. When she discreetly glanced his way twenty minutes later after Mabel told them dinner was ready, the glass appeared to be just as full, though the man holding it still brooded.

The family went into the dining room since Mabel insisted that the large room off of the kitchen get put to use again. No one bothered to argue with her.

The evening meal continued in the same vein as the minutes prior and to Brenna's mind, the time depleted too quickly. Obvious disappointment and a little awkwardness hovered over the meal when Eliza asked if Brenna was looking forward to the annual Halloween party at the ranch. Eliza assumed her brother had mentioned it.

"The Peak puts on the town's Halloween party each year. Our folks started it and we didn't see any reason to stop."

Brenna shook her head in regret. When she informed them that she would be riding into town with Ethan and Gabriel in the morning, all eyes turned to Ethan. He offered them stony silence and an outward shrug.

At the meal's end, Ethan retreated to the front porch. Eliza, however, followed Brenna upstairs and asked if she could speak with her a moment.

"Of course, come in." She stepped aside and followed Eliza into the guest room.

Eliza looked around the room. "I haven't been inside this room since Rachel."

"Who's Rachel?"

Eliza immediately grimaced, further piquing Brenna's curiosity. They'd formed a kinship after Eliza's initial response to Brenna's relation to Hunter, and Brenna knew her meddling came from a place of love.

"Brenna, I think you and I need to have a little girl talk." Eliza sat down on the edge of the large bed and motioned for Brenna to join her. "Just bear in mind that I shouldn't be telling you any of this."

Brenna couldn't stop the smile from forming on her full lips. "Why, then, are you telling me?"

Eliza sobered. "Because I like you and because I love my brother. Now don't interrupt until I'm done."

She nodded and made herself comfortable.

"About five years ago a family came through here by the name of Davis. They had a daughter, Rachel. She was my age at the time, but she and Ethan took to each other. They ended up spending a lot of time together and got along quite well. Ethan didn't love her, that much we all knew, but he did care for her, and he took the idea of responsibility seriously enough to consider marriage.

"When her parents informed her that they planned to move to California, Ethan thought he'd ask her to marry him. She agreed and her parents seemed delighted with the match. Rachel moved in here since her parents planned to leave the following week. They wanted Rachel to have a long engagement and would return in three months for the wedding."

Eliza stopped for a moment and listened as though she may have heard something. She shook her head but continued. "About two weeks into the engagement, I heard Ethan and Gabriel arguing in the library.

Of course I eavesdropped, and it turned out that they argued about Rachel. Gabriel claimed he walked in on her and one of the hands rolling around in the hay together. Ethan denied that Rachel would do such a thing since they were officially engaged, but Gabriel was adamant. I remember they didn't speak for a while after that."

Brenna leaned forward, and her hands gripped the folds of her skirt.

"Another month passed and they began preparations for the wedding. Ethan was having a difficult time sleeping one night while I'd been up reading in the library. I heard him leave the house. Sometimes he likes to go swimming when he can't sleep. I went out onto the porch to speak with him when I noticed he switched directions.

"It was about that time when I saw a light on in the barn. I followed Ethan. I walked up right behind him and was about to say his name when I saw what he was looking at."

"Rachel."

Eliza nodded. "Yes. She and the same

hand who Gabriel mentioned before, lay half naked in one of the stalls, and they stared up at Ethan. He didn't even say anything. He just turned around, acted as though I wasn't there, and left the stable. I didn't see him again that night. The next morning, Gabriel drove Rachel into town to stay at the boarding house, and she caught the stage two days later. The ranch hand hightailed it that night."

Brenna welcomed the unexpected anger. "I would have hit her, I know I would have."

Eliza sheepishly confessed her own sin. "Actually I did hit her—hard. No one asked why she had a black eye the next day."

Brenna tilted her head and smiled at her new friend. "I believe I really like you, Eliza Gallagher."

"And I believe I really like you, Brenna Cameron."

Brenna instantly sobered. "Why did you tell me this?"

Eliza sighed and moved to stand next to the bed facing Brenna. "I told you because I do like you and I love my brother. I don't know what happened between the two of you out there, but something did. Since you've been back, the only two blind fools walking around are you and my stubborn-headed brother. I can see how much Ethan cares for you, but he won't be the first one to say anything, that much I know. He's too full of pride and distrust from Rachel. It's been a lot of years since she left, but the experience left Ethan with a sour note about commitment. You telling him that you planned to leave probably only made him angry. Angry enough that he'll try to just push you right out of his mind."

"You said he didn't love her," Brenna reminded her.

"He didn't, but it doesn't take away the betrayal, or his stubbornness." She hugged Brenna and parted with, "Just think on what I said before you ride into town in the morning."

Eliza left the room, closing the door softly behind her until it clicked. Brenna understood betrayal too. Betrayal from the people she loved most in her life, people she trusted.

Brenna found falling asleep difficult. She thought her days of confusion were behind her, but it turned out there was more going through her mind now than when she first stepped off that stage. She flung the bedding off and slipped her soft cotton robe around her shoulders, covering the matching white nightgown that reached her from neck to ankles. Brenna put on a pair of heavy socks to ward off the chill from outside and quietly slipped down the stairs and onto the front porch. Nothing but darkness surrounded her. She could barely make out some of the noise coming from the bunkhouse. It seemed as though some of the boys ended up in a long card game. Otherwise only the sounds of the night kept her company as she walked the front length of the wide porch.

Brenna didn't want to leave this place tomorrow and thought back on what Eliza told her. *Does Ethan care for me?* Brenna couldn't lie to herself and say she cared nothing for him. She loved the man. She trusted him with her life, and her father had been the only one she felt that safe with before. Before she discovered his lies. *Can I really be the first one to say something?*

Deep in thought, Brenna didn't hear the sound of crunching rocks until it was too late to do anything about it. A rough hand came around her and covered her mouth to prevent any screams, while another hand forced her back up against a rank-smelling body. Brenna attempted to push it away, but she wasn't strong enough to kick the man away from her. Another man, his lower face covered with a cloth, came around the front of her and tied her hands and feet, then slipped a gag around her mouth. The pathetic yelp she managed earned her a quick bash to the head.

"You didn't have to hit her."

"Shut up and get her on the horse."

The culprits looked around making sure that no one heard and rode off into the night with Brenna lying face down in front of Bradford James.

12

"I do believe I'll join you for these games more often, little brother."

"You do and I'll be out of my share of the ranch in no time."

The brothers shared their good humor as they walked back from the bunkhouse in the darkness. Ethan had let some of his frustrations out by beating up on his brother in the stable after dinner. He had found him there checking on one of the geldings who had cut its leg on a rock two days ago.

It didn't take long for Gabriel to realize what his brother wanted, and he was happy to accommodate him. When both of them fell over, tired and dirty and unable to exert any more energy, they laughed.

"Feeling better?"

"Actually, no, but at least now I'm too tired to care about it," Ethan said with a half scowl, half grin.

"In that case why don't you join the boys and me for that game?"

"Don't mind if I do."

That ended Gabriel's winning streak, but since his brother seemed to be in slightly better spirits, he had no complaints about the lost money.

Just when they reached the steps of the porch, Ethan stopped.

"What's wrong?"

Ethan shook his head and held up a hand to silence his brother.

A strange and foreign sensation, deep inside of him, couldn't be shaken. Panic slowly settled in as he recognized the feeling as emptiness. The only reason he could possibly be feeling that is if Brenna was gone.

Ethan pushed his brother aside and raced inside. He took the stairs two at a time, Gabriel fast on his heels, and didn't stop until he reached the Brenna's room.

Ethan opened the door and hurried to the bed. He swore swiftly and loudly and looked up at his brother. Gabriel knew it before Ethan said anything.

"She's probably around here somewhere, Ethan. Just calm down."

But neither brother believed it, not really. Eliza walked into the room, rubbing the sleep from her eyes. ready to yell at the offenders who woke her up from a pleasant dream. She took one look at her brothers and the empty bed, then changed her mind.

"Did you hear anything, Liza?"

"Not a thing."

Calmly, Gabriel placed a hand on his brother's shoulder. "Let's search the house and then outside. She can't be far. All of her things are still here."

"We would have seen her outside." But even as he said it, Ethan left the bedroom and went downstairs while Gabriel searched the upper rooms. A few minutes later, Eliza was dressed and helping Ethan search downstairs. Mabel heard the commotion and rumbled into the kitchen.

Gabriel checked the front yard while Ethan took the back. Everyone ended up in the kitchen empty-handed, except for Gabriel.

"What is it?"

Gabriel saw the deep-rooted fear in his brother's eyes. He held out a small scrap of white cotton and lace. Ethan grabbed it and the question reached his eyes.

"It hung from a loose nail on one of the front railings and caught about waist high."

Ethan shook his head as if to clear it of all other thoughts. He lifted his face and stared at his brother with eyes dark enough to appear dead. "Wake the men and meet me in the stable."

Gabriel headed for the bunkhouse. Eliza caught up with them inside the stable and saddled her mare. Less than fifteen minutes later every ranch hand at Hawk's Peak had saddled and mounted their horses.

Ethan's stallion moved restlessly, catching onto the unusual mood of his rider.

"Jake, Ben, and Tom, you ride north and spread out. Pete, Kevin, and Tom Jr., you ride south. Carl and Henry and Eliza, you take the western tracts. Gabriel and Colton ride with me."

Everyone bolted from the ranch in all directions. Ethan rode hard to the east, not looking back to make sure that the others followed. He cared only about finding Brenna. *I can't lose her*, he kept thinking. He had let his stubbornness and pride prevent him from telling her how he felt, even though he admitted it to himself.

The same thoughts continued to echo in his mind. *Please keep her safe. I can't lose her now.*

13

Brenna didn't think her head ever hurt as much as it did at that moment. She raised a hand only to find both of them tied together. At least they tied her hands in front of her body. Shaking her head in an attempt to clear the fog from her mind, Brenna waited until her eyes focused and looked around. She was in some kind of shack with a dingy cot on one side and a wooden stand with a basin of water on the other. She lay precariously on the edge of the cot over dingy sheets.

Brenna groaned with the effort of sitting up, pausing when she began to feel lightheaded. Her feet weren't tied together, small favor though it was. She needed to relieve herself and her throat hurt and felt parched. Brenna made awkward use of the chamber pot in the corner, thankful it was empty. Shabby though it appeared, the shack was free of excess dust and stench, which meant that it was probably used often. She went to the small barred door, but her futile attempts to open it failed. It seemed to be locked from the outside.

Brenna searched the rest of the small space but found no cracks, holes, or loose boards. Dejectedly, she sat back down on the cot and waited while the damp cold of the bare floor seeped through the thick stockings on her feet. Brenna didn't have long to wait.

Two voices mingled quietly outside, and she heard the bar scrape against the door as someone lifted and set it aside. The door opened to a tall, broad-shouldered man, though not nearly as tall as the Gallagher men. He stepped inside with a plate of food and smiled down at Brenna. She wanted to retch. She recognized the man from the first day she arrived in Briarwood. Bradford James.

The man offered her the plate of food. Though Brenna felt a slight rawness in her stomach, she refused the victuals. Brenna wasn't sure how long she'd been tied up, but from what she could see outside the door, it appeared to be morning.

"Don't want the food, huh? Well that's all right because I'm not much in the mood for eating." With a sick laugh, Bradford closed the door and moved toward her where she sat on the cot. Brenna immediately stood and moved to the opposite side. She couldn't go far.

"You didn't really think that Gallagher would get to keep you all to himself now, did you?" he said, whining in a sick, pathetic voice.

"How did you know I'd returned to the ranch?" Brenna was desperate to keep him occupied.

Bradford sneered. "You didn't think we wouldn't be watching you, did you? You're mighty important to someone."

Brenna's body shuddered involuntarily. There was only one person in the area who she knew hated her, but she couldn't imagine why her grandfather would do something so drastic as kidnap her. He had told her that he never wanted to see her.

"I don't know why you've taken me, but I'm warning you right now to stay away." Her eyes flashed angrily and Bradford whooped and hollered, enjoying every moment.

"I do like that sweet accent of yours. You know I never had me a Scot." He slowly removed his coat followed by his belt and shirt. Brenna backed into a corner.

"You won't get away with this."

"If you don't fight me, I'll make it nice and painless for you. I'm betting you've never been with a real man, am I right? Well I'll make sure it's real special for you." He began removing his breeches when the door flew open.

"Get your clothes back on and leave her alone."

Brenna could see only the outline of the unexpected man as the sun shone directly behind him.

"I was promised her and I'm just

collecting."

"When the job is done you can have her. Not until." The other man waited until Bradford picked up his discarded clothing and left the shack. The moment the door closed with the bar in place, Brenna shook with relief.

Hours later, the men of Hawk's Peak all circled back around to the ranch. No one found any sign. Ethan, Gabriel, and Colton rode out to the Double Bar. Ethan had been so sure that Nathan Hunter was behind this, but when he reached the ranch, they found only a few workers and a handful of whores. One of the men told them that Hunter stayed in town with some of the men.

In his gut he knew Hunter was involved, but even with the hatred he felt for his granddaughter, Ethan couldn't figure out what good would come of kidnapping her.

"There's no sign of her," said Pete.

"Nothing to the west either." Eliza moved her mare next to her brothers. "At least nothing that seemed out of the ordinary. What about Hunter's place?"

Gabriel shook his head. "Not a damn thing, but I have to agree with Ethan on this. I'm willing to bet the ranch that Hunter is behind this."

"But why?" Eliza asked.

"Ramsey," Ethan said.

Ethan motioned his brother and sister closer to the group. He told the men to head back to the ranch for food and to water the horses. He wanted everyone ready to go back out again.

"Elizabeth confessed a little something to me when Brenna wasn't around. Elizabeth brought a substantial fortune to her marriage. There was never any doubt that Hunter married her for the money, but Elizabeth's father attached a stipulation to her inheritance. If Elizabeth died, nothing went to her husband, only their children or grandchildren."

"That would explain why he tried to find her after she disappeared, but he still had Ramsey with him at that time," said Eliza.

Ethan leaned forward in his saddle. "Yes, but Ramsey stayed because of his grandmother, and I'm sure Hunter knew that."

"So he thinks to use Brenna to draw out his grandson?" Gabriel asked in disbelief. "I don't see how that could help his cause. They aren't going to stay with the old man. How would he know that Brenna even knows where her grandmother is or if Ramsey is even alive?"

"He could kill them." Eliza's soft words brought both brothers' attention to her. "If he got his hands on Brenna, he could use that as a threat against the rest of them. A life for the money. I don't know if Ramsey is alive, but don't you think Elizabeth would come back to save her granddaughter?"

Ethan nodded. "I know she would." He shook his head, not knowing or having any other answers and for a brief moment, he felt helpless. He spurred his stallion forward and yelled over his shoulder. "Back to the ranch."

The rest of the men waited by the corral, guns and horses ready. Ethan and the others rode up hard and fast.

"I want everyone to listen carefully. I still believe that Hunter is behind this, but I won't risk anything happening to Brenna." He turned to four of his men. "Pete, Kevin, Jake, Tom, I want you to ride up north and ride hard. Pack enough gear for a couple of days. Take the north trail around Devil's Crest. Stop only for the horses' sake and nothing else. Tom Jr. and Carl, ride out and keep a discreet eye on the Double Bar in case any of these mongrels decide to ride back in. Henry, ride into Briarwood and wire for the marshal. I believe he's in Wyoming for a trial. Tell him to get out here as fast as he can. Then come back here and keep an eye on the place. I don't trust them not to double back. Ben, you'll ride with us. Eliza, I want you to stay here with Mabel.

"Ethan, don't you dare ask me to—"

"Eliza, no arguments." He used that tone in the rare times he pulled family rank. She didn't have to like it, but she wouldn't ignore it.

Pete pulled up alongside Ethan. "Where exactly up north are we going, and where do we meet up?"

"You're going to Desperate Creek. If we're not there in four days, bring Elizabeth Hunter back here." More than one shocked face stared back at him, but no one argued or questioned Ethan's orders.

14

They bound her feet and gagged her once more. They threw her awkwardly onto a saddle, this time sitting up and in front of someone. She guessed it was the man who stopped Bradford James from taking her in the shack earlier. Brenna stiffened as he pulled her body tightly against him and told the men to head out, and they fell into place behind the lead rider.

"Relax, Miss Cameron. You won't be any good to yourself if you remain stiff like that."

The voice did belong to the man from the shack, but now it sounded almost kind. She turned and looked at him. He could be considered a good-looking man with blond hair and blue eyes. He didn't look like someone who rode with filthy men.

"Ah, I can see you want answers, but that won't do you any good right now. Just relax and this will all be over soon."

Brenna attempted to speak, but everything came out muffled.

"If you promise not to scream, I will remove the gag. If you do scream, I will be forced to silence you. Agreed?"

Brenna nodded and stretched her jaw when he removed the cloth.

"Why have you taken me? I deserve to at least know that much."

"You know the location of something that someone else desires," he answered calmly.

"That's impossible. I've been in the territory for only two weeks."

The man smiled. "Yes, but you have done and seen much in that time, haven't you? I can see that you are still confused, so I will explain. During the time that you went away with your Gallagher, you met a special person, didn't you?"

Brenna's eyes grew wide.

"I see you understand now. This special person has been lost for some time, and it is important to my employer that she be returned."

Brenna wanted to spit in his face. She had never spit at anyone. "I will never tell you where she is, never."

"Ah, I believe I told you not to yell or I may have to silence you, but I really don't want to bruise that pretty face." Instead he tied the gag back around her face and whispered in her ear. "You will see that I do not wish you harm. I am merely here to do a job. You have been promised to James as a reward, but I will try to help you escape afterward if you cooperate."

A muffled "never" made it through the gag and the man laughed.

"You have spirit but careful it is not misused."

Brenna closed her eyes and fell half asleep in the saddle, her body rigid. They rode for hours and didn't stop until darkness fell upon them. Her unknown riding companion pulled her down from the top of the horse and carried her to a fallen log.

"I will remove the bindings on your feet, but it will not do you any good to run. There are many unpleasant things in these woods." With one swift action, he cut through the rope around her ankles and replaced the large blade in a sheath at his side. He removed the gag and laughed.

"You may scream all you like tonight for no one would hear you." He stood up and brushed the dust from his pants.

"You could at least tell me your name." Brenna cringed as the feeling rushed back into her legs.

The man looked at her thoughtfully for a moment. "Just call me Jack."

Brenna scoffed at Jack's retreating back. When the numbness left her body, she took a few minutes to study her surroundings. Excitement suddenly welled up inside of her. The men stopped near the same location she and Ethan had camped the first night when she saw the black bear. Of course Brenna didn't know her way around, but she just might be able to find her way back, or perhaps up to

Bright River. The town was too far, but she might be able to make it to Hawk's Peak. She remembered that the first day consisted of small hills and woods, nothing she couldn't handle on foot. That is if the cold and animals didn't kill her.

Brenna looked down at herself. Her once white cotton nightgown and robe were dust-covered and smudged with dirt from being held against dirty men. The thick stockings she had put on her feet might protect her against small twigs, but nothing sharp or too hard. *Well, what was a pair of feet when it meant freedom?* She remembered Ethan saying that this trail led directly to Bright River with a cut off for wagons heading west past Desperate Creek.

Jack brought over a plate of beans and bread and loosened the ropes on her hands enough for her to eat.

"Why are we going to Desperate Creek?" Brenna decided to chance it and she got lucky. The man looked genuinely surprised.

"How did you know where we travel?"

She shrugged. "Nathan Hunter is your employer, is he not? It's he who is looking for my grandmother." Brenna played a risky bet, but it continued to pay off.

Jack didn't look pleased. "You know too much. I wonder, which of the men told you all of this?"

"No one told me, you don't seem to be very good at your job, *Jack*." Perhaps I've gone too far, she thought. "The only thing I don't know is how he found out, and if he does know, what does he need with me?"

Jack shrugged his heavy shoulders. "You know too much already, so what is a little more? I followed you." At her surprised look, he let out a deep, disturbing laugh.

"Not the whole time of course. I arrived in Bright River before you, and it was easy enough to find out where you went from there. I wired my employer to let him know, and he kept James there watching over at Hawk's Peak until you returned."

"You're rather free with your information all of a sudden. Do you intend to kill me?" Brenna needed to find a way out of this fast, but she also didn't want to put her grandmother in danger.

He gave her another irritating shrug. "I told you I will keep you safe until this is over, but you will belong to James. I can do nothing about that. Perhaps I will even enjoy you myself."

"You said you would help me."

"Yes, well you are a beautiful woman, and I see no reason not to find a little more pleasure in this job. Perhaps I will have you first."

With that said, Jack left Brenna feeling sick and desperate. She wasn't about to cry or lose control in front of these disgusting men. Oh, how much I need Ethan now, she thought.

Jack forgot to tighten her hands back up when he left. She ignored the food and set the plate on the ground. The men obviously thought she'd be no trouble because they kept their backs turned to her and spoke quietly with each other. It was now or never.

"What's your plan?" Colton asked Ethan as they all crouched down behind a thick line of trees. They finally caught up to Hunter's band. They must have thought no one followed because their campfire was easy enough to find just off the trail.

"I'd like nothing better than to go in firing and kill every last one of them." Ethan's voice was low and angry, but thankfully in control. "But I won't risk Brenna that way."

"Then we have to get her out first," said Gabriel.

Ethan nodded in agreement. "Ben, I want you to go around to the west side of the camp, Gabriel to the east. Colton, you stay here and cover my back. I'm going in to speak with them."

"Now wait a minute—"

"Gabe, not now. I have to get her out of there."

"Okay, we'll play this out your way."

Ben started toward the west side but came back. In a low whisper said, "She's not there."

"What?" Ethan moved over to the opening he used earlier and looked to the log where Brenna had been speaking with one of the men. His eyes scanned the camp but found no sign of her. One of the men looked up and shouted to the rest. He recognized the voice belonging to Bradford James.

"Shit." The low expletive was muffled by the wind. Ethan returned to the other three.

"Ben's right, she's gone." Ethan swore again and ran a hand roughly over his face. "All right, Ben and Gabriel go to the west side as planned and see if you can find her. I'll skirt around to the north. Colton, you stay here in case she heads this way. Just be careful of these miscreants. They'll shoot anything out here that moves."

Silently the foursome split, doing their best to avoid the other men searching.

She was able to move silently, but she could still feel the sharp rocks and twigs breaking through the thick fabric on her feet and digging into her flesh. Brenna gained enough of a head start, but her bound hands made the escape more difficult.

She knew the moment when they

discovered her missing. The shouts went up in the camp, and she clung desperately to her nightclothes to avoid tripping over them.

Brenna knew she hadn't run far and wanted desperately to cry when she ran right into a heavy male chest. Even in the darkness she knew a stranger held her, and she fought him with everything she had in her. It took her a moment to realize that he was trying to speak to her. Only then did she recognize him from the ranch.

"Calm down, Miss Brenna. It's all right." He put his arms around her body, forcing her own arms to her sides. She struggled a bit more when she saw another man run up in front of her. He took her in his arms and held on. Brenna's mind recognized him before her eyes did, and she managed to relax.

"It's all right, just take it easy." Gabriel forced her to look at him. "Listen to me; we have to get out of here. Can you run?"

She no longer cared about her damaged feet. "Yes."

Gabriel took her hand and the three of them ran. He would have preferred to wrangle the lowlifes in, but getting Brenna to safety held priority. They barely managed to avoid Hunter's men and met back where Colton waited.

Brenna felt a rush of panic. "Where's Ethan?"

"He went to the north. When we saw that you had left, we weren't sure which way you might have gone." Gabriel untied her hands and rubbed warmth into her arms. "I'm going to get Ethan. Stay here with Colton and Ben."

Brenna nodded and let herself be folded into Colton's warm coat. Gabriel stood to leave when a gunshot fired. It came from north of the camp.

"Son of a bitch!" Gabriel disappeared, not waiting for anyone else.

Colton turned to Ben. "Take Brenna and ride to the ranch. Don't stop for anyone." Colton handed her care over to Ben and raced off after Gabriel.

"We have to leave now, Miss Brenna." Ben half carried her and lifted her onto the back of his horse and climbed up behind her. He urged the large animal into motion. They rode for only about a mile when Brenna asked him to stop.

"We can't leave them, Ben, please. We have to go back."

He shook his head. "I have to get you back to the Peak, ma'am."

"Listen to me. Those men are going after my grandmother. If you won't take me back to them, please take me to her."

"Ma'am, listen, we're still two days of hard riding away from Desperate Creek. Ethan sent men up there and they'd be there soon now. I have to get you back to the ranch." He made it clear he wasn't going to argue with her any more.

Ben put the horse in motion once more and when they reached familiar land, Ben spurred the gelding into a run. They reached the ranch by first light, and when they approached, Eliza and Henry ran toward them. Henry lifted Brenna into his arms and carried her inside. Eliza followed and Ben left his horse to Tommy. Mabel rushed into the sitting room where Henry gently set Brenna down on the sofa. Mabel sent Ben to fetch her home medicines and hot water.

"Please tell me you're all right." Eliza sat on the sofa next to her legs.

"I am, I promise. Could I please have some water?" Brenna's voice felt hoarse, and she heard how raspy it sounded. She ignored both food and water since being kidnapped and the effects began to hit her full force.

Eliza went to the sideboard and poured her a glass of water. While Brenna took slow sips, Eliza turned her attention to Ben. "What happened?"

"We caught up to Hunter's men, but Brenna slipped away just before we could go into camp. We split up and that's when Gabriel and I found her."

"Ethan and Colton?"

"Ethan went north of the camp, Colton stayed south. We brought Brenna back, but we heard a gunshot. Gabriel and Colton ran in the direction of the shot, and Colton told me to bring Brenna back here. I'm sorry, I just don't know what's happened to them. I'm going to saddle another mount and go back out there."

"No." Henry put an arm on Ben's shoulder. "You stay here and rest up. I'll go out there, just tell me in which direction."

Ben nodded. "We left them on the north trail that goes up into Bright River. They were camped near Ruby Creek where the paths diverge."

Henry turned to leave but Eliza stopped him. "I'm going with you."

"No." Brenna reached for Eliza's hand.

"I have to." The force of Eliza's words told Brenna she was serious, but Brenna had to convince her otherwise.

Brenna lifted her head slightly to look directly into the other woman's eyes. "No. Please wait and listen before you get angry. I know they ran off because they thought Ethan might have been shot. If he was, they'll bring him back here, won't they? Ethan would never forgive himself if you were hurt on his account and you know it. Please don't put that burden on him."

Brenna's gentle pleading worked. She

used the one weapon Eliza would respond to—her family's safety.

"Fine, but if they aren't back by nightfall, I'm going out."

Ben set his hat on the back of a chair. "Once Miss Cameron is settled, I'll head back into town and see if there's word from the marshal."

Mabel, with her medicines and large bowl of hot water in hand, pulled off Brenna's socks.

"My goodness child, what have you done?" Mabel obviously didn't expect an answer because she set to tending the feet and wrapped them with long strips of white cotton. Ben carried her up to her room before he left the ranch, and Eliza remained with her until Brenna went to sleep.

15

Brenna slept for what felt like days and awakened to the sound of voices. She did her best to erase the grogginess from her mind and looked around. She could see only shadows in the dark room. It appeared to be the dead of night. The voices sounded muffled, but she could tell that both men and women spoke. Brenna donned a wool wrapper over her long blue nightgown, unsure how she came to be wearing it, and went out into the hall, cringing at the pain that shot up from her bandaged feet. Brenna ignored the pain when she saw the light coming from Ethan's bedroom down the opposite hall.

A sudden anxiety built up in her and she ran on her padded feet to the doorway.

Colton, Ben, and Eliza stood at the base of the bed. Gabriel sat on one side and Mabel on the other. Brenna walked into the room. Gabriel saw her first, and rushed to her side.

"Brenna, you really shouldn't be in here right now," he said.

"Ethan. What's happened to him?" She tried to look around Gabriel, but he blocked her view.

"Ben went for the doctor, but it's going to be a little while before he can get out here."

"What happened?" Her near shout captured everyone's attention. Eliza came forward with tears in her eyes.

"No! Tell me he's going to be all right."

"We just don't know anything right now," said Eliza.

"Don't you dare send me away, Gabriel, not now."

He studied her face for a moment, then nodded and released her. She immediately went to the bed.

Mabel hunched over Ethan and set some kind of poultice on his bare shoulder.

"He's lost a lot of blood," said Mabel, "a lot of blood. That doctor better get himself here and fast." She grumbled for a few more minutes and tried to get a dark liquid down Ethan's throat. Gabriel finally helped her since Ethan lay unconscious. Mabel sat up from the bed and turned to the others.

"I can't do anything more. That doctor's going to have to remove that bullet."

Gabriel and Eliza absently nodded and thanked Mabel.

"What now?" Brenna whispered.

"We wait." Gabriel slammed his fist on top of the dresser. "He shouldn't have been out there alone."

"What happened?" This question came from Eliza who moved to sit next to her brother on the bed.

Gabriel let out a long deep sigh and looked at Ethan. "After we heard the shot, Colton and I went to the north end of the camp where Ethan had gone. He slit the throat of one man, but another came right up behind him and shot him in the back. We managed to get two of them, but the third got away."

"There were five." Brenna glanced up at Gabriel.

"Five? We saw only four of them in the clearing."

"I'm certain there were five. Bradford James among them."

"Yeah, that's the throat Ethan slit. Shit, I don't know where the other could be. Excuse me, Brenna." He hook his sweat dampened head. "What in the hell is keeping Ben and the doc?"

As if they knew they'd been summoned, Ben and the doctor rode up to the ranch less than ten minutes later. The doctor maneuvered everyone out of the bedroom except Mabel. Two hours later, Eliza dozed in a chair in the sitting room. Everyone else paced and waited. Brenna didn't bother to change out of her nightclothes and no one seemed to care about anything other than what was happening upstairs.

"There has to be something . . ." Gabriel's frustration didn't ebb and he remembered what brought about this whole mess.

Before he could say anything more, the sound of riders interrupted everyone. Gabriel was joined by the others on the front porch and waited as Henry and four other riders came up.

"I'm Marshal Wallis." The man sitting atop a tall silver gelding stared down at them. He was a large man dressed entirely in black except for the silver star on his breast. Gabriel knew he took over the job of marshal last month, but he hadn't met the man yet.

"Henry's filled us in as best he could, but me and my deputies will need the rest of the story."

Gabriel shook the marshal's hand. "We'll tell you everything that we know, but it's become more complicated. My brother's been shot. The doc is up with him now. We have two of the kidnappers, one's dead up in the hills, and two got away."

Gabriel took the marshal and his deputies out to the barn where they left the two men tied up. Gabriel turned around and spoke in a low voice to Ben who immediately nodded and headed for the stable. Henry went with the other men while Eliza and Brenna went back inside.

Brenna regretted not telling Ethan she loved him, and now she feared she may never get the chance.

The men sent to bring Elizabeth back to the ranch arrived in the early morning hours, and Brenna felt such relief at seeing her grandmother once more. She found comfort in the older woman's arms.

"I worried for you, Grandmother." Brenna held the other woman closely. "They weren't certain you'd be safe."

Elizabeth stepped back just enough to bring a hand up to Brenna's face. "My darling child, it is lovely to see you and thank you."

"For what?"

"For embracing me as you did."

Brenna pulled her grandmother back into her arms and said, "You're my family. I will always embrace you as such. You are well?"

"I am, though I must say these men surprised me," Elizabeth said.

"You'll stay?" Brenna asked. "At least for a visit."

"I shouldn't. I know Ethan brought me here to keep me safe, but I don't believe it will be safe for you." Elizabeth softened the refusal with a smile. "As far as everyone in these parts are concerned, except those at this ranch, I'm long dead. I want them to continue thinking that, at least until my husband is gone."

Brenna nodded. "I understand, though I long for the day when you no longer feel the need to hide from him."

"I believe that day will come, but not yet." Elizabeth turned when Eliza came upon them. "You're as lovely as you ever were, Eliza, perhaps lovelier."

"My brothers would disagree with you," Eliza said with a faint smile.

"Ethan sent the men after me," said Elizabeth. "I'd like to thank him."

Brenna and Eliza went silent and Elizabeth saw the tears in Brenna's bright eyes. "What's wrong?"

"Ethan has been shot," Eliza said, but was quick to add, "He'll make it."

Brenna raised her eyes to Ethan's sister. Eliza nodded with greater conviction. "He'll make it through. Ethan is too stubborn to die before any of us."

Another two hours passed and still nothing from upstairs. The marshal and two of his men left for the Hunter ranch, and the other two escorted the kidnappers to the jail in Briarwood.

By early morning light, just as Brenna began to fall asleep on the settee, Mabel walked into the room. Everyone stood and waited silently for the news, good or bad. She said nothing and turned as the doctor came in behind her. The man looked worn out and wore a grim expression.

"He pulled through." A collective rush of relief coursed through everyone in the room but the doctor held his hand up. "It's going to be touch and go for the next couple of days. He's lost a lot of blood."

"But will he live?" asked Gabriel.

"I'm surprised he's lived through this much, but he's strong. He has a good chance."

Gabriel thanked and paid the doctor,

and Ben hitched up the wagon and gave the doc a ride back into town.

"Now I want you to go up and get some sleep, all of you. There's nothing you can do for him right now." Mabel wouldn't relent until Eliza and Gabriel went up to bed. Brenna however refused and went to sit with Ethan.

"Brenna?" The voice sounded raspy, but it breathed life. Brenna moved from the chair to the side of the bed and took Ethan's hand.

"Yes, I'm here."

He tried to raise his hand and touch her face. He felt incredibly weak and his shoulder throbbed. Brenna poured him a glass of water from the pitcher next to the bed and held it for him while he drank.

She softly caressed the side of his face and smiled through her tears. "You're going to be just fine, Ethan."

Brenna left the bed and went into the hall. Her shouts brought everyone within hearing distance to the bedroom. It was a joyous occasion as everyone spoke at once.

He's going to live, she thought. *He must live.*

She returned to his bedside and less than five minutes later, Ethan sank back into sleep.

Ethan began to heal nicely. When the doctor visited a week after he removed the bullet, he happily informed everyone that Ethan would make a full recovery. Brenna declined to leave his side other than when absolutely necessary. During those times, either Mabel or one of the family members relieved her. It comforted her to watch Ethan regain his strength. After the first week ended, and the doctor told him he'd mended well, Ethan's body and disposition undertook a drastic improvement. A couple of days later, he left the bed and began walking, though a bit stiffly at first.

Brenna set aside the idea of leaving and hoped she would never have to. Ethan was on the mend, but he still had a while yet before he could resume ranch duties. When the family talked about cancelling the Halloween celebration, Ethan insisted that the party should still take place, if for no other reason than to honor their parents' tradition.

Brenna tried once again to convince her grandmother to stay.

"Please understand that I must leave now."

"I do, Grandmother," Brenna said. "But I will miss you."

"We'll see each other again." Elizabeth smiled and held Brenna's hand. "Like you said, we're family."

Brenna lowered her gaze and pulled her grandmother into her arms for an embrace.

"My dear child," Elizabeth said softly. "You're not staying?"

Brenna shook her head. "I don't know yet."

Elizabeth lifted Brenna's chin and smiled at her. "You will try?"

Brenna nodded. "Yes, I will try, but if I must leave, know that you are always in my heart and that I will see you again."

"You promise, dear?"

"I do, Grandmother."

The Halloween celebration was a festive occasion that celebrated the time between the falling of leaves and the cold winds of winter. Gabriel told Brenna that they didn't usually see snow in these parts until November, though they've been surprised by winter as early as September. The Halloween gathering was one of the last times most of the ranchers and farmers who lived far from town got together before they settled in for a long winter.

Brenna had been sorry to see her grandmother return to Desperate Creek, and no matter how much everyone tried to convince her to stay, Elizabeth insisted on leaving. She wasn't ready for everyone to know she lived. Brenna believed her grandmother had grown accustomed to hiding and the fear of coming back overwhelmed her. But Brenna worried more for her safety. She didn't believe that her grandfather would stop looking for his wife now that he knew she was alive. Unfortunately, no one had been able to find Nathan Hunter since her kidnapping, and the marshal wanted proof of Hunter's involvement before he spent resources looking for him.

Brenna would have already been on a ship if she left when planned. Ethan had yet to say anything to her other than the occasional small talk, and Brenna's heart filled with trepidation.

One morning she asked Ben to send a telegram for her while he was in town. When he returned the next day, he handed her another telegram.

"Good news, I hope."

Brenna glanced up at Ben and managed to mimic his smile. "Good enough. Thank you for delivering this."

He tilted his head and continued to smile, but Brenna saw the worry in his eyes.

"You're sure everything is all right?"

Brenna nodded. "Of course." She smiled again, though her heart didn't mean it. The same outfit that sent out the last ship she inquired about planned to send out one more to England before the winter. It would be a cold journey, but they had a cabin available if she wanted passage. She would reply and ask the captain to hold a space for her, but she held out hope that Ethan may ask her to stay.

The idea of making another journey on her own seemed daunting this time, but she wouldn't ask a stranger to accompany her back to Scotland. Images of Iain and Maggie entered her mind, and Brenna realized just how much she missed them and her home. She would make the journey again alone or perhaps the private detective she hired to find her grandfather could find a companion for her—someone she could trust. She did her best not to think about the difficult decisions she may be faced with making. With hope in her heart that there was yet a chance with Ethan, Brenna tucked the telegram away in the pocket of her skirt and went to find Mabel to ask if she could help with the party preparations.

The day of the party approached and it seemed to Brenna that the entire town of Briarwood made an appearance. A few canvas tents were set up with fire pits, and stoves were placed far enough way to not cause a fire. A warm spell hit, bringing cool winds rather than cold, and the sun shone brightly enough that everyone seemed to enjoy the autumn day. They temporarily transformed the large barn into a dance hall. A band of talented townspeople had been assembled and the guitar, fiddle, and voice of a local townsman blended in joyful tones. Couples danced in formations Brenna didn't recognize, but they appeared to have a grand time. Eliza pointed out some of the more complicated steps, and Brenna delighted when the band played a familiar jib. Plenty of food was offered: beef, corn, beans, potatoes, cobblers, peaches, meat and fruit pies, tarts, punch, and a special supply of brandy.

Ethan felt almost normal, with the exception of the sling the doc told him to wear. Brenna turned herself out in her favorite dress—one she made for the last Christmas party she went to with her father. It was a deep green, with matching lace along the collar and hem. The cut was more formal than what one might expect for a country dance, but Mabel assured her she looked perfect for the occasion. Her striking red hair had been washed, rinsed with rose water, and brushed until the heavy curls shined. She pulled it only partway back with a black sparkling clasp, leaving the rest of the long curls to float around her shoulders and down her back. She left her neck and wrists bare of jewels, and realized she'd not thought to bring them out since her arrival.

When she made her appearance, Brenna turned more than a few heads. Ethan and Gabriel stood near the front porch when she stepped outside. Her smile intensified when Gabriel gave her an appreciative look and a charming grin. Her eyes found Ethan and she faltered momentarily. He looked . . . angry. *Why on earth would he be angry with me?*

His scowl grew when Gabriel took Brenna's hand and led her out into the throng of unfamiliar faces.

The evening turned out to be a

whirlwind of eating, dancing, and laughing. She danced with Gabriel as well as Colton, Ben, Henry, and Carl, the only ones brave enough to ask. It was a night for her to remember, though not quite complete.

Ethan watched her the entire evening. He knew she wasn't like Rachel, and he hadn't loved Rachel, but he couldn't help but convince himself that there were similarities. Rachel came into town and not long after that Ethan found himself engaged. It didn't take long for Rachel to find comfort in another man's arms. He didn't believe that Brenna dallied with any of his men, and he knew his brother hadn't touched her. *Why is she laughing and flirting with every man here?* She seemed to be so comfortable around his brother that she didn't pull away when Gabriel laid an innocent hand on her shoulder or back.

Ethan ignored the fact that Gabriel behaved no differently than he ever did with Eliza, but Brenna definitely wasn't his sister. He stiffened a little when

Gabriel left Brenna in the arms of the doc and walked over to stand next to Ethan on the outskirts of the celebrating.

"Are you planning on scowling at her all night or are you going to ask her to dance?" Gabriel glanced back and forth between his brother and the party.

"Don't you have something better to do right now, Gabriel?"

"Can't think of a thing." His brother seemed undaunted by Ethan's surly attitude. "You have always been the one to give me advice and I've always looked up to you, but God strike me down if I *ever* behave the way you have since you brought her home."

Ethan wanted to walk away, but something in what Gabriel said forced him to stay put and listen. He waited for Gabriel to say something else, but the look on his brother's face told him he wasn't going to. Gabriel wasn't looking at him any longer but just off to the side of the house. Ethan followed his gaze and wanted to curse the day he'd been born. *How in the hell can this be happening to me right now?* His eyes flew immediately to Brenna who continued with her dance.

Gabriel's gaze also flitted over to Brenna. "Do you want me to handle this?"

Ethan shook his head. "I'll take care of it, but I don't know what in the hell she's doing here. It's been five years."

"I'll stay with Brenna." All other disagreements and disputes aside, Gabriel was on his brother's side. He just prayed that things wouldn't get out of hand. Eliza intercepted him as the current dance ended.

"What has you looking so uneasy, Gabe?" Her brother jerked his head behind him toward Ethan.

"Why that bitch." Eliza never swore and it caught Gabriel off guard. "I can't believe this. What is she doing here?"

"I don't know. She just rode up in that fancy buggy."

Gabriel stopped his sister when she started toward her brother who now argued with the woman.

"Let Ethan handle it," he said firmly and turned his attention back to locating

Brenna. "Shit." Eliza also saw Brenna and thought the same thing.

Brenna's eyes once again had gone to the spot by the porch that Ethan previously occupied. When she didn't see him, her heart jumped a few quick beats until her eyes scanned the area and found him again. He spoke with a woman near the house, a smartly-dressed and attractive woman. From this distance, Brenna could tell that she was tall and slender, her expensive clothes well fitted. She couldn't see Ethan's face, but the woman didn't smile, that much she could tell.

Gabriel and Eliza didn't reach Brenna in time and saw her walk toward Ethan. Gabriel let out a low expletive and followed.

Brenna arrived just in time to realize the identity of the woman.

"Ethan, darling, how could you think of sending me away? We were, after all, engaged to be married."

Brenna stopped just behind Ethan who didn't yet realize she stood there. The woman, however, noticed her and offered her a condescending scowl.

"And who might you be?"

Ethan slowly turned around.

Brenna ignored him and answered the woman. "Brenna Cameron."

The accent caught the woman off guard, as it did most people, but she quickly composed herself and placed an obviously practiced smile on her face.

"Delightful. I am Rachel Davis, Ethan's fiancée."

She turned her eyes briefly to Ethan who had stepped forward. "She's not my fiancée, Brenna."

"Oh, Ethan." Rachel set her hand on his shoulder though her eyes focused on Brenna. "After all we shared, you know you can't mean that."

"What are doing here, Rachel?" Eliza asked, tired of her act.

"Your brother and I have some unfinished business, and it really doesn't concern you."

Gabriel wanted to hit the woman. Instead he pulled his sister back and draped an arm over Brenna's shoulders. "I believe we have a party to get back to." He had to use a bit of pressure on her shoulders to get Brenna to move. He gave his brother a hard look.

"Brenna, wait," Ethan said.

They stopped and Brenna turned to look between Ethan and Rachel. He said nothing else, so she left with Gabriel and Eliza.

"Who is she? Rachel did her best to draw his attention back to her.

"None of your damn business. Now for the last time, tell me what you're doing here." Ethan wanted nothing more than to go after Brenna, but Rachel needed to go first.

"Now that really isn't any way to treat the woman you loved."

"For the love of—that was over five years ago. You couldn't possibly have thought that when I threw you off this ranch that I meant for you to come back." Ethan shoved the hand away that she tried to keep putting on his arm. He couldn't imagine what brought Rachel back to

Hawk's Peak or why she seemed desperate to reunite. Rachel disgusted him, but she was a beautiful woman with a wealthy father. If a quick marriage was what she wanted, there were smarter choices.

"I hoped—"

"Well you hoped wrong. Now get off of this land before I throw you off."

She stalled. "Please just allow me stay the night." Her frantic pleas sickened Ethan. "I left home and I have nowhere else to go. I just need a place to rest and I'll leave on the next stage out, I promise. I could stay at the cottage."

Ethan snorted. "You aren't exactly good at keeping promises now, are you? And that cottage is for family only, so don't even think about it."

"I promise, just tonight."

At that moment, Gabriel returned to stand by his brother, though it wasn't with a smile. "I'm surprised you're still here." Gabriel cast Ethan a look that lacked brotherly warmth.

"Ethan offered to let me stay for the night. It is, after all, too late to return to town."

Ethan didn't want Rachel to stay any more than the rest of them, but they began to draw too much attention. Hoisting the unwanted baggage into her carriage and forcibly removing her from the ranch would draw too much attention, though Ethan was tempted.

"Just for the night, but tomorrow you leave." He feared she was about to jump right into one of her melodramas and held up his hand. "I don't want to hear anything from you because I don't care about your problems. One night," he reiterated, then turned and left his brother standing alone with Rachel.

Later that evening, when the last guest left and all the food was eaten from the plates, the men cleared away the tents and stoves and made sure nothing else remained that might draw the local wildlife.

Gabriel joined the boys for a late night game, though he confessed to his sister that he didn't want to chance seeing Rachel again that night. Eliza kept to her room, too angry with Ethan to speak to him. Brenna found comfort curled up on a large chair in the library with a novel in hand. Although the book lay open on her lap for almost twenty minutes, she had yet to turn a page. Her heart knew that Ethan didn't deliberately invite the woman here, but it still hurt to see him with a woman to whom he once proposed marriage. It was far more than he thought to do for her. Perhaps she just expected too much from him. Maybe a part of him still cared for this Davis woman despite what Eliza told her. It required too much thinking, and Brenna was weary.

She rose to put the borrowed novel back in its place on the shelf and retired to her room.

Gabriel left the card game early to join his brother on the porch. He thought he'd quit poker and see how he could do with talking some sense into Ethan.

"I love you, Ethan, I always have and always will. I want you to be happy, but lately you're just angry. The thing is, there have been moments since Brenna first arrived that I saw you smile in a way that you haven't in a long time."

"I haven't heard anything out of her that makes me believe she wants anything to do with me." Ethan's voice softened, but his hard gaze faced the far pasture on the other side of the pond.

"That's because you're a stubborn idiot."

"You're all heart." Ethan shifted his position so that he stood facing his brother.

"She's afraid."

"Oh, well, since you're now the expert on women, what exactly is she afraid of?"

"Same thing you are, I imagine. She doesn't want to admit her feelings and be rejected. She's been through a lot."

"You're so sure she loves me, huh?" Ethan scoffed at the idea, but Gabriel didn't miss the desperate hope that crept into his brother's eyes.

"I know you love her, and I know she's hurting, but she's survived too much to wallow in self-pity. She's not Rachel."

Ethan's gaze met his brother's with the

intention of telling him to mind his own business, but he couldn't. His brother was right—again.

"This place, it means too much to me. There have been other women, you know that, but they all resented the time this ranch took away from them. This is a hard life for most women, but someone like Brenna . . . she's strong, but is it fair to ask her to give up her life for mine? I honestly don't know what to do."

"Well that's because you haven't spent enough time studying the fine art of finessing women."

Ethan found a chuckle from somewhere within. "You do enough of that for the both us."

"Perhaps." Gabriel acquiesced. "Rachel showing up now was just bad luck, very bad luck, but you have to forget about her and realize what you're about to lose."

Ethan nodded absently, but said nothing.

Gabriel squeezed his shoulder. "Just think about it. By the way, why did Rachel come back?"

"Hell if I know."

"She did like to stir up trouble. If you don't want to talk to her, I can. Either way, you better see to it that whatever brought her back isn't going to be an issue."

Ethan nodded. "I'll talk to her, and if that doesn't work, I'll put her and Eliza alone in a room together."

Gabriel's laughter followed him into the house.

The night grew chilly after the sun set, but the light cotton nightgown Brenna wore kept her warm enough. She slipped out of bed thinking that she would sneak down to the kitchen and warm some milk, though the thought of sleeping under the same roof as Rachel kept her awake. Outside in the hall, Brenna stopped at the top of the stairs. Halfway up stood Ethan, staring at her.

Ethan's entire body tightened. Her hair fell long and loose down her back, and she looked like a wanton angel. Her nightgown was barely noticeable in the darkness, but her face drew him in. He half expected her to leave and return to the safety of her room, but she didn't move. Ethan slowly ascended the stairs but Brenna remained.

What is she doing? Ethan wanted to ask her. *Didn't she know how dangerous it was to be around him?*

Brenna couldn't get her feet to listen to her brain. She remained rooted at the top of the stairs. When Ethan reached the step just below the landing, she could feel the warmth radiating from him. His sling blended with the stark white shirt he wore. He had long ago discarded the gray wool jacket from the party.

Ethan reached out and ran the back side of his hand slowly across her cheek, back and forth.

"Ah, you shouldn't be here." He trailed his fingers down her neck.

"I was going downstairs to get some milk." Her voice halted when his fingers caressed the back of her neck.

"Turn away now while I can still let you."

Brenna raised her head to meet his eyes and in that moment, she knew she could never deny this man anything. It didn't matter that his former fiancée slept down the hall or that she might be on the next stage east. Only right now mattered. This man, this night. "I don't want you to let me." She leaned into him.

Her soft simple words broke down the last of his resistances. All of the hours she stayed by his side while he healed rushed back to him. All of those same hours that he tried to push her out of his mind and heart knowing that she planned to leave. *How can I think that she is anything like Rachel?*

Saying nothing, Ethan took her hand and pulled her back to the guest room. He wanted her in his bed, but this room was on the opposite side of the hall from the family's rooms and from their unwanted guest. Brenna followed silently into the bedroom and stood in the center of the room as Ethan closed the door behind him and joined her.

He lowered his head close to her ear and said in a voice that caused her entire body to shiver, "One last chance, Brenna, because after this, there's no turning back."

Brenna looked into his eyes and knew that marriage or not, she would rather spend one night in the arms of this man than a lifetime of never knowing his touch.

In answer to his last statement, Brenna cupped his cheek in her small soft hands and rose onto her toes, pulling him toward her until her lips barely touched his.

With a low groan, Ethan put his one good arm around her, pulled her tightly against him, and deepened her kiss until nothing innocent remained between them. He removed the sling from his arm, lifted her to his chest, and guided her over to the large poster bed, laying her gently in the middle of the feather mattress. Other than the light seeping through the windows from the sliver of moon, darkness cloaked the room. Just enough light to see her red swollen lips and half-lidded eyes.

The anticipation drove Brenna mad. She didn't know what she needed or wanted but she knew only Ethan could give it to her. With his arms holding her tightly, Brenna closed her eyes and gave herself to the man she loved. No hesitations. No regrets.

The following morning Brenna woke to a cold bed. Sometime during the night, Ethan had left her alone. She wiped the sleep from her eyes as the soreness in her legs reminded her of what had happened. She went to the washbasin in the corner to sponge herself down and quickly dressed and plaited her hair, leaving the braid to fall down her back. She needed to find Ethan.

The quiet halls welcomed her, and when she listened, no sound drifted to her ears except for the melody of Mabel's singing from the kitchen. The sun shone brightly in the sky and a quick glance at the clock told Brenna that the morning meal had come and passed.

In the kitchen, Mabel rolled out heavy rounds of dough but turned around with a cheerful smile when Brenna entered.

"Well good morning. Quite a party,

wasn't it?"

Brenna nodded and smiled. "Yes, quite." Brenna's thoughts focused on the hours after.

"Have a seat, I saved you some breakfast." Mabel set a plate of bacon, biscuits, and flapjacks in front of Brenna and poured her a fresh cup of tea. Mabel obviously noticed her dislike of coffee.

"It's quiet this morning." Brenna sampled the fare, which was delicious as usual.

"Oh, well, the men are all out on the range. Lots of fences need mending before the first snowfall. Eliza's off with the breeding mare and that other woman is around here somewhere."

With everything that transpired the night before, Brenna nearly forgot about Rachel. "And Ethan and Gabriel? Are they with the men as well?" She looked at her nearly empty plate. Apparently she had more of an appetite that she thought.

"Those two rode into town. Should be gone most of the day." Mabel said nothing else as she formed the dough and slid the loaves into the hot oven.

Brenna took her plate and cup to the sink and thanked Mabel for the breakfast.

"Oh, wait a minute there," Mabel called out to her.

Brenna turned around from the doorway and faced Mabel.

"Ben tells me that you sent a wire to book passage on a ship. He said you'd have to leave tomorrow."

Brenna's stomach turned and her heart ached. She'd forgotten about the ship and leaving—not forgotten entirely, just hoping someone gave her reason to stay. She would have to send a telegram to the private detective about hiring her a traveling companion. This morning she'd felt such hope and she wanted to speak with Ethan. Surely he will ask me to stay, she thought, or perhaps I'll ask him.

"I did, but I'm not certain that I'll be leaving tomorrow. I'll know more this evening."

Mabel shook her head and clucked her tongue. "It sure would be a real shame for you to leave the Peak. It's been real nice to have another woman around the place to keep Eliza and me company. The winter days get lonely." She shook her head again and returned to her baking. "Yes you will be missed."

Brenna nodded absently and left the kitchen. *Tomorrow. Will I have to leave?* Brenna prayed with all of her heart that the panic she felt was for naught, but she must speak with Ethan. She went out onto the front porch and held her arms tightly around her chest. It seemed the cool days traded places with the cold for the duration of the winter season, but it wasn't too cold for a ride. Ben came whistling by with a large ax in hand, and Brenna called out to him.

"Well, good morning, Miss Brenna." Ben tipped his hat and walked over to stand by the steps.

"Good morning, Ben. Chopping wood today?" She indicated the ax.

"Yep, a few of us will be cutting and chopping for the next week to finish filling the extra woodshed before the snow."

She nodded as though she agreed to

something, but Ben didn't seem to notice.

"Do you happen to know what took Ethan and his brother into town today? It's just that I have to speak with them, and I thought I'd ride into town if someone could join me."

Ben pulled his heavy coat a little tighter around his chest as a cold breeze whipped past, but he didn't appear too affected.

"Sure, they went in to meet with some of the mining men about a cattle purchase, I believe."

It seemed that Mabel wasn't the only one who knew what went on at the ranch.

Ben thought to add, "I'd be happy to take you, but I don't think you should be riding to Briarwood to meet them. I'm not right certain where their meeting is, and you'd probably miss them."

"Thank you, I'll wait."

Ben tipped his hat once again. "Good day." He walked off in the direction of the barn.

The day stretched on, and Brenna spent most of it helping Mabel gather the last of the autumn vegetables from the garden for canning. She managed to avoid Rachel the entire morning and most of the early afternoon. Unfortunately her luck wasn't to last. Brenna found herself back in the library when the door opened behind her.

"What exactly do you think you're going to get out of Ethan anyway?"

The cool feminine voice came from behind Brenna. She turned to see Rachel just inside of the doorway. I really hate this woman, she thought. Brenna didn't care that the hate damaged her soul, she just hated her. "You speak in riddles, Miss Davis."

"Of course you know what I mean." Rachel glided into the room, smoothing the bodice of her dress. Her smile conveyed no warmth. "If you're waiting around for him to fall at your feet and propose marriage, you're wasting your time. He'll be marrying me, I assure you of that."

"Oh, and what gives you such confidence?"

"Well, now it wouldn't be fair to tell you before I tell Ethan, but I suppose that it might help you to see how fruitless your efforts are. Ethan and I were more than just an engaged couple, if you understand my meaning."

Perhaps before last night she may not have, but Brenna feared she knew exactly what Rachel meant. *It couldn't be true, could it?* Ethan wouldn't have shared this woman's bed. Then again, they had been engaged, which is more than Brenna could say for herself.

Rachel's smile grew and it sickened Brenna. "You see, Ethan left me with more than just a night to remember. We have a child and that isn't something Ethan will turn away from."

Brenna's eyes opened wide in disbelief. "Why haven't you come forward with this before now?"

Rachel shrugged. "My father wouldn't allow me, of course. I was young and naïve and so I stayed with my family until I could finally get away."

Perhaps others fell for her lies, but Brenna wasn't the gullible type.

"I admit it's a remarkable story, Miss

Davis, and at first I almost believed it."

Rachel faltered. "It doesn't matter if you believe it or not. It's true and you'll learn soon enough that Ethan won't turn his own child away."

"Oh, I don't doubt that." Brenna walked slowly toward the taller woman. "Ethan is the most honorable man I know and would never abandon his own flesh and blood, but you're forgetting something rather important. Ethan wasn't the only one who knew of your indiscretions during the time you stayed at Hawk's Peak. If there is a child, I truly doubt it belongs to Ethan."

Brenna now stood only a foot away from Rachel. The other woman looked as though she wanted to hit her, but Brenna knew she was stronger and angry enough to stop her.

"How dare you, you little tramp." Rachel lifted her hand as though to slap Brenna when a hard voice yelled out from the doorway.

"Don't even try it, Rachel, or we'll both discover that I'm not the lady my brothers think I am." Eliza stepped into the room and pulled Rachel's extended arm back. They stood equal in height, but the long days of hard work on the ranch made Eliza strong and fit. "I don't care how you do it, but you get yourself and your things out of here now."

"Your brother won't stand for this." Rachel seemed to forget her guise.

Eliza laughed and stepped away to stand by Brenna. "You know, I actually think he'll thank me for it. Now go." Rachel nearly ran from the room.

Brenna turned to Eliza. "How long had you been standing there?"

"Long enough to hear her filthy lies. Thank you for not believing what she said about her and Ethan. I doubt my brother ever touched her in that way."

Brenna sighed with relief. "Actually, I believe they could have been intimate, but I didn't believe the rest. Though I'd be a fool to believe anything that woman said."

When the sounds of a wagon rolling in reached Brenna's ears, it took great effort not to jump up and go out to meet Ethan.

Eliza gave Brenna an encouraging smile and went out front to meet her brothers. Mabel announced dinner and Brenna didn't see Ethan until he and Gabriel ambled into the dining room. He took a seat across from her and only briefly met her gaze.

Her heart sank. *What did I expect?*

"Uh, not that I'm not glad to see her gone, but where's Rachel?"

Brenna glanced at Eliza but said nothing.

Eliza sat down next to Ethan. "Rachel has a pressing engagement and will leave tonight. She's packing her things now."

Ethan stared at his sister but let the matter drop.

The evening meal filled with lively chatter, mostly from Gabriel and Mabel. Ethan joined in when the talk turned to the contract they'd set up that day with the mining company.

Sometime after dinner, Brenna sat in the guest room on the edge of the bed. She changed over an hour ago and after she brushed her hair until her scalp hurt. Eliza retired directly after the meal and Gabriel joined the boys at the bunkhouse for a game of cards. Brenna waited until she heard Ethan's familiar footsteps on the stairs.

She opened her door and stood just under the threshold. Ethan stopped at the landing and after a moment's hesitation walked over to her. His eyes remained cool and Brenna felt a sudden chill. What happened since supper to make him so angry? she wondered.

"Eliza told me about what Rachel said. Thank you for not believing her."

Brenna knew that wasn't what bothered Ethan but nodded just the same. "Did you ever . . . touch her in that way?"

Ethan stared at her with his deep blue eyes, and she saw the truth in them.

"Please, don't answer that. How do you know she's not speaking the truth?"

"She's conniving enough to have come after me long before now. I never imagined she'd be desperate enough to come back."

"Did you love her?" Brenna spoke the

words but dreaded the answer.

"Never. I made a mistake, one of the worst of my life." Ethan stepped forward, but still kept distance between them. "I spoke with her before I came in here. I sent a telegram to San Francisco to see what I could learn about her reasons for coming. It seems she does have a child, too young to even belong to the ranch hand she dallied with here. Her parents didn't know she was here. They've lost the bulk of their wealth. Otherwise, her father would have bought her a husband."

"She believed you would marry her and accept the child." Brenna looked up at him. "I don't blame her for trying, though I do wonder why she waited all these years."

Ethan returned her stare. "Desperate people do desperate things. I was going to marry her once, and perhaps that still meant something to her." Ethan moved like he was going to reach out, but he slid his hands into his pockets instead. "I have never fathered a child, Brenna, and I certainly wouldn't marry her if I had. Call me dishonorable if you want, but I couldn't do it, not when I know the type of person she really is. But I would not turn away from a child who was mine."

Brenna found comfort in his declaration. Even now she wondered if it was possible she could be with child. She also knew that if she said the words, he would do the honorable thing by her, but did she have the courage to say the words first, or to accept a man who only declared himself because of honor?

Ethan appeared to become restless. "Ben told me that he's taking you into town tomorrow to catch the stage."

"Well, yes, I mean perhaps."

"Which is it?"

He wasn't going to make this easy.

"Ethan, what happened last night—"

"Shouldn't have happened. I'm sorry for it. I shouldn't have let things get so out of hand."

A slap across the face would have been preferable to his words. The bold temper she inherited from her warring Scottish ancestors surfaced. "You weren't alone, if you'll remember, and I don't recall stopping you."

"That's true." He leaned back stiffly against the railing.

"So that's it? It shouldn't have happened?"

Instead of answering her, he asked her a question. "Do you want to leave?"

It dawned on her in that moment that he wasn't going to declare his love. He wouldn't beg her to stay and marry him. Perhaps she expected too much from him. She should have listened to Eliza when she tried to warn her about Ethan's past and his distrust of women. But Brenna wouldn't beg for a man who felt uncertain about her, no matter how she wanted him.

"I want you to care enough and give up that stubborn pride of yours long enough to realize that I don't want to leave." Brenna waited and hoped. Could he really be so damaged? she wondered and wished she found it in herself to hit Rachel before she left.

"I do care. More than I've ever cared for anyone."

Brenna studied him closely and realized he was scared.

"You won't ask me, will you?" *He's not ready.*

"Brenna, I . . ."

She stepped forward and placed a finger on his lips. "You know where I'll be. When you're ready, you know where I'll be."

"You could stay. You have family here now."

She shook her head and smiled softly, feeling everything all at once. She needed to get away while she still carried the strength to let him go. Perhaps I'm the foolish one, she thought. But she knew the only way to love Ethan, without having him as her own, was to get as far away as possible. I'm not giving up on you, she promised silently. Don't give up on us.

"I have family—in Scotland."

Ethan nodded and when he spoke his voice sounded hollow. "Well, then, safe journey."

16

"Are you sure you know what you're doing Brenna?" Gabriel stood in the bedroom doorway next to his sister.

"No, but I'm doing it anyway." She placed the last of her items in the trunk.

"The ocean crossing can't possibly be safe this time of year," said Gabriel.

"I wired to Boston and found a ship heading to England. They make the crossing this time every year, but I must leave today if I'm going to make it in time."

"You can't go alone, either." Gabriel took hold of her hand. "It's not safe."

"I arrived alone in one piece." Brenna moved her hand out from under his. "But you don't have to worry about that. The private detective who helped me find my grandfather has found me traveling companions. An older couple who are returning home to England. We'll meet in St. Louis and make the journey together."

"Don't go. Whatever it is can be worked out," Eliza said.

"I just can't." She hated the desperation she heard in her voice. "I can't. Please don't ask me to."

"I knew my brother behaved stupidly about this, but I never thought I'd use the same word for you."

Brenna slowly turned until she faced Gabriel. "You're the brother I never had and always wanted, but I'm still leaving." She set her satchel on the stack of trunks and looked around the room one last time.

"What happened with Rachel, you can't believe it meant anything," said Eliza. "She left this morning, she's gone."

"I don't, not really." Brenna did her best to lessen the melancholy tone she heard in her own voice. "It's Ethan who can't forget and let it go. I know too much of pain and loss to be the one who forces his hand. He has to want me enough to let go of the past, and I don't want him until he does." Brenna took a long, deep breath. "Ethan's healed enough and back to work. My grandmother is safe, thanks to your men catching Jack and Hunter's other man by surprise. My grandfather has disappeared, and there's no hope for justice right now. Everyone is safe, and it's time I left. I have the answers I came looking for, or at least most of them, so please trust me to know what I'm doing."

Gabriel lifted a hand to her face. "Do you really know what you're doing?"

Brenna tried to prevent the tears from falling. "I'm giving us a chance, in the only way I know how."

"He'll come around, and you won't be here," Eliza said. "You'll regret that. You both will."

"I will never regret anything about Ethan."

"What about your brother?"

Brenna sensed Eliza's reluctance to let her go and regretted that she was going to disappoint her. "I'll find him, I know I will, but I'll have to do it from Scotland."

"That would take much longer." Eliza walked around the foot of the bed to stand next to Brenna.

"Then it will take longer."

"But your family is here." Gabriel forced her chin up with his finger.

"My grandmother understands." Brenna tried to pull away before he saw the tears forming in her eyes.

"That's not what I meant."

A soft knock sounded at the door. Henry stood there holding his hat.

"Ben has the wagon hitched to take you into town. I came to bring your trunks down."

"Thank you," Brenna said softly and turned back to the others. "Good-bye."

Henry set the hat on his head and she followed behind him as he carried two of her trunks down the hall, but then she stopped and placed a hand on the door.

In a whisper so soft he barely heard the words, she said to Gabriel, "Please tell him good-bye for me."

The blow to his head came unexpectedly.

Ethan had spent nearly two weeks recovering from his last injury, but his arm and shoulder still ached every time he flung the ax or lifted a bale of hay. He wasn't expecting to add a headache to his list of injuries. It would have been difficult to fell a man Ethan's size, but Gabriel was big enough to do the job.

"You're a jackass." Gabriel stood over Ethan who struggled for a moment to get up.

"What in the hell did you do that for?" Ethan rolled his shoulder slightly to make sure that it wasn't damaged and turned on his brother.

"You know exactly what it's for. Now I don't know what kind of reason you could have possibly given yourself for letting her go, but you did it. I know you love her, which is why I can't understand why you're behaving like such an idiot." He had finished shoving his brother around, but the desire to go another round remained.

"It's none of your business, so stay out of it."

"She's like a sister to me and if any man

ever treated Eliza the way you did Brenna, you know for certain the man wouldn't be able to walk after we finished with him. So what in the hell makes you so special?"

Gabriel faced him with the same look he used to have when they were about to brawl, but this time, Ethan sensed Gabriel's disappointment more than his anger. They drew a bit of a crowd and the hands not out with the cattle gathered nearby.

Ethan felt like he'd been run over by a herd of stampeding longhorns, and he imagined he looked as bad. His shoulder was on the mend, but sleep eluded him and he hadn't cared enough about his appearance to shave in a few days.

Gabriel took a step closer and placed a heavy hand on Ethan's shoulder.

"I don't know what happened between the two of you, but I've seen the same pain I'm seeing in your eyes."

"And where was that?"

"In Brenna's eyes the day she left."

Ethan met his brother's gaze.

"I think Brenna believes you're too beat

down by women that you could never give her what either of you wants. If that's true, then let her go and put her out of your mind. But if it's not true, you should kick yourself every day for the rest of your life for letting her go."

"Don't you think I know that?"

"Then go to her. Set your pride aside long enough to realize what you've lost. Forget the past, and let go of your fears for the future. Brenna would make a life here if it meant being with you—I believe that. Go to her."

"And you think she'll forgive me? Just like that?"

"Hell, no, she'll probably kick you right back out."

Ethan slapped his brother's shoulder and looked up at him with the first hint of a smile that he'd seen in weeks.

"When did you become such a sentimental ass?"

Gabriel laughed. "I don't know, but it's scaring the hell out of me."

Ethan gazed across the land he called home and would until the day he died. He always found solace here. Now he felt something missing. *Did I not tell myself to stop running? I admitted to myself that I loved Brenna. Then when the opportunity presented itself to tell her, I did exactly what I said I wouldn't do. I ran. I dishonored her, betrayed her trust, and ran.* Ethan gave his brother one last look and went to the house. He just prayed it wasn't too late to fix the wrong done to her.

17

In the countryside of Borthwick, Edinburghshire, Scotland Spring 1883

Spring held a special place in Brenna's heart. A beautiful season when she and her parents tended the gardens or a mare bore a new foal in the stable. The crisp cool air caressed her skin as she walked along the banks of the pond near her home. The large stone manor house that rose grandly on twenty acres of beautiful green pasture and rolling hills on the outskirts of Edinburgh would be cleaned and polished from top to bottom every spring and again in the autumn. It was a refreshing time of year, and a time of new beginnings and growth.

Brenna didn't want this year to be any different, but deep down she knew that nothing in her life would ever be the same.

"I hope ye aren't planning on riding her, lass," Iain said with his thick brogue and eyed her suspiciously as he filled the feeder with fresh oats. He worried about his sweet lass. She walked around with a distant look in her eyes ever since she returned home. He'd never seen her as unhappy as she looked now.

Oh, how I long to sit on the back of Heather and race across the countryside. Brenna could nearly feel the cool breeze whipping through her hair as she imagined riding her mare.

"No, I'm not, so don't go worrying about it." The mare nuzzled her mistress's hands and Brenna laughed, holding out a sugar cube. "Though how I have missed her."

"We thought ye'd be sending for her seeing as how ye said ye weren't coming back." Iain had always been there for her family, and she knew he worried. When she came home unexpectedly, he immediately asked what happened. Brenna told him of her condition and when he asked about the father, she hedged. She refused to tell him a thing. He had always been like an uncle to her and always a joy to have around, but this she couldn't share with anyone.

"Things change. I was wrong to leave Scotland." She would never regret it— couldn't regret it. She had more than just herself to think about now. Brenna pulled her heavy cloak together as she left the warmth of the stable and slowly walked back to the house. The spring air nipped at her face and she looked around at the first hint of life in the gardens and the nearly full greenhouse. She wondered how long it would be until she could no longer bend over to pull a few weeds.

Iain came up behind her and gently took her elbow. "Why don't ye go on inside and rest, lass? I'll have Maggie bring ye some hot stew."

"I'm pregnant, Iain, not ill."

"I know, but yer father, God rest his soul, would haunt me to my last breath if I let anything happen to ye or the wee one."

Conceding to the older man, if for no other reason than to placate him, Brenna went into the house and directly to her room. Maggie brought a tray of hot stew as promised, thick black bread, and creamy goat's milk. Even though she just ate her morning meal three hours ago, Brenna quickly consumed the delicious meal.

She looked at the empty tray and tenderly patted her growing stomach. "With all the extra food I eat, I imagine you'll be big and strong when you come out." *Just like your father.* Brenna believed with all of her heart that the child growing within her would be a son, and the sudden remembrance of the night they conceived him rushed back to her like a fierce wind over the cliffs. Lately, she only thought about Ethan when she was awake and he no longer haunted her dreams, but it took her hours to fall asleep because her thoughts always turned to him.

She had discovered her condition on the journey to England. Luckily, the captain and older couple with whom she traveled thought she had a weak constitution and couldn't handle the motions of the sea. Brenna spent the majority of her time closed away in her cabin. Ironically, once they docked, she no longer became ill, causing her to think that perhaps she might not be pregnant after all. Then on the journey north to Scotland, she realized it wasn't to be and deep inside she felt grateful—happy even—because she wanted a part of Ethan by which to remember him.

Brenna spent the remaining days of winter and early spring at home with Iain and Maggie for company. She avoided the city ever since her condition became apparent to old friends and acquaintances. Brenna could have told everyone that she had just been married and widowed in that short time, but she didn't care and refrained from lying about something she couldn't regret. She planned to live her quiet life and imagined the day when she might return to him.

A soft knock sounded on her bedroom door. Thinking that it must be Maggie coming to take her tray, she simply told her to come in.

Brenna looked up from her comfortable chair in front of the fire and felt her chest tighten. Her skin tingled and her hands seemed to shake on their own. The shock prevented her from saying anything for some moments.

Ethan stood there in the threshold, looking big, strong, tired, and more handsome than she remembered. Brenna said nothing, and remained in the chair with a heavy afghan over her lap to hide her growing stomach.

"How did you get inside?" She realized the question a stupid one, but she could think of nothing else to say. Her heart lurched and pounded rapidly. *Please remain calm.* She couldn't however, ignore how her body and heart responded to his presence.

Ethan stepped into the room holding his fancy black hat at his side. He was dressed in a clean black suit, though slightly rumpled. The disheveled appearance only enhanced his appeal. "I asked the old man—Iain, I think he said his name was—where I could find you. He looked me up and down and asked if I was the father and what took me so long to get here."

Brenna gasped and Ethan took a few more steps until he stood in front of her. In one quick movement, he pulled the afghan away from her and stared down at the evidence of their one night of shared love and passion.

Ethan's eyes revealed his pain as he met hers. "Did you plan to ever tell me?"

Brenna forced the tears to remain hidden, but the mist in her eyes betrayed what she felt. "I don't know." Even though her pride begged her not to, she asked, "Why did you come?"

"Why in the hell do you think I came here?"

Anger coursed through her body. She stood as swiftly as she could and held her small frame as largely as she could, which was a pathetic undertaking when she stood next to him. Pride prevented her from backing down.

"I don't know why the *hell* you came

here, but I will thank you to turn yourself back around and leave." Brenna tried to storm for the door, but he grabbed her arm, forcing her to stop.

"That's my child too. I won't be denied my rights. If you want me to leave, the child goes with me."

Brenna whirled on him and brought her hand across his face. "How dare you come here after you turned me away only to now demand that I give up my baby. I'll tell you right now, Ethan Gallagher, that this child is going nowhere."

He released her arm and stepped away.

"Then neither am I."

Ethan's soft promise frightened her more than any outburst could have. She rushed from the room, her dignity and pride bruised. *Ooh, that stubborn, infuriating man!*

She now breathed normally, slowly. She felt in control of her emotions—somewhat anyway—and the implications of what it meant for Ethan to have come swarmed through her mind. He hadn't known about the baby before he left Montana, so that wasn't the reason.

Could it be that he still cares about me, even after I left him?

She wouldn't bemoan the circumstances of her life. There was no going back to undo the past. She wouldn't change a thing, even the trying times, for they, too, led her to this point. She refused to give up the child for anything or anyone. Brenna planned to make the best out of Ethan's presence in her home and stay as far away from him as possible.

Well, she hadn't kicked me out of her house which said something, Ethan thought. Then again, Ethan didn't give her much of a choice. It wasn't the reunion he planned in his mind on the grueling ship crossing. He'd been lucky to find passage on the first cargo ship set to sail in the spring. The exorbitant price charged by the captain was a small price to pay in order to reach Scotland sooner than a passenger ship would have allowed. Only the future mattered and in his future he wanted Brenna by his side for the rest of his days. If he must remain in Scotland, he would stay.

The possibility that he might not return to Montana tore at his soul but not nearly as much as losing Brenna forever. He risked that once, and he would not give up without trying to win her back. Perhaps Gabriel was right about her willingness to settle in Montana. He didn't deserve it now, which is why he was willing to remain in her home, but if there was a chance she might return, he would grasp it.

Ethan believed it would take every minute of his time there to convince Brenna that he could make her happy— that marrying him was the best choice, the only choice. Breaking wild mustangs was going to be child's play compared to this new task he'd settled on himself. With a new outlook, Ethan went in search of Iain.

He found him in the stable after a long search of the beautiful grounds. Different from Hawk's Peak but just as lovely. Ethan found that if he had to live away from his ranch, he could make due in

Brenna's world. If a choice needed to be made, his choice was Brenna. *A child! We are going to have a child.* Ethan walked quietly into the stable, but it seemed that Iain could hear just as good as Mabel. *Shouldn't that deteriorate with age?*

"I wondered if I'd see ye again," Iain said in his thick brogue, which Ethan barely understood. Iain brushed down a beautiful silver-grey mare that Ethan would love to buy for his sister, though he doubted Brenna could be convinced to sell him the animal.

"She's a beauty." Ethan stepped up to the other side of the mare.

"Aye, she is that, just like her mistress."

"This is Brenna's mount?" Ethan shouldn't have been surprised.

"That she is. Heather is her pride and joy. Her father gave the mare to Brenna when she was little more than a young lass." Iain slowly ran the soft brush across the mare's coat. He didn't seem like a man who ever hurried. Ethan admired that.

"Well, I suppose ye're stayin' on for a spell then?" Iain showed no outward emotion as his eyes turned to Ethan.

Ethan nodded. "For a spell."

"Ye couldn't have known about the bairn, so why have ye come?" Iain stopped brushing Heather before he asked his last question and waited patiently for Ethan to answer.

"I came for Brenna."

The firm, resolved statement convinced Iain that Ethan told the truth.

"Ye broke her heart, lad," the old man stated disapprovingly, "and it won't be easy to be mending."

"I know, but I'm going to keep her, one way or another."

Iain shook his head and moved around the mare and told Ethan to follow him. The old man took Ethan on a short walk through the woods where they ended up at one of the most beautiful lakes Ethan had ever seen.

"This is one of Brenna's special places. She says it's the best place to think in Scotland. She came here after her mother died and again after she lost her father." Iain chanced a look at Ethan and saw the younger man deep in thought, gazing over the glistening water.

"She's been coming here often since she returned home."

Ethan turned his eyes from the view and faced Iain as the old man spoke to him, his brogue firm and unyielding. "My Brenna has been hurt enough for two lifetimes, but I'm believing that she still cares for ye. I dinna know who the father of her bairn was, but I could see in her eyes she missed him something fierce. Now ye listen here, lad, it will be Brenna's choice to go with ye or not. Now I can see that ye're hurting just like she is, and if the two of ye would stop acting like idjuts, ye just might realize it." Iain felt a soft raindrop on his cheek and turned up to the sky and smiled. "Ye know lad, when a soft rain falls on Scottish soil, which is all of the time mind ye, it leaves behind a land more beautiful than before. It's a cleansing for the land. Aye, Scotland is a place for healing. Even those who don't stay long are reborn."

Ethan stood under the rain and smiled as Iain slowly walked back toward the house. Ethan removed his hat and lifted his face to the sky, letting the rain course over his tanned skin. Mabel would sometimes spin anecdotes like the one he'd just heard. *There was hope.* And if Iain hadn't booted him out for what he did to Brenna, there was hope indeed.

Brenna remained conspicuously absent from the meal that evening. Maggie told him that her mistress didn't feel well and preferred to dine in her room. Ethan might have worried, given Brenna's condition, but he seriously doubted that her sequestered state had anything to do with her pregnancy and everything to do with avoiding him. He wasn't going to let this daunt him. He enjoyed a leisurely supper with Iain, where the old man regaled him with the history of Cameron Manor.

Brenna's ancestors had built the manor, and her family lived within the stone walls for centuries. Ethan understood the importance of a legacy. To think she might have been willing to give it all up for him humbled him. His guilt weighed as it should for not declaring himself when he first had the chance. Pride was sin enough, but fear—there was no excuse for it.

Ethan thanked Maggie for the superb feast, then joined Iain for a brandy.

The following morning found Ethan breakfasting alone. Iain had gone out to the stable an hour before, and Brenna once again took her meal upstairs. Ethan worried for about one minute before his worry turned to irritation. Ethan would give her a few more days before he barged into her room once more. Although, he had to reason, that would hardly bring him closer to his goal of winning her back.

Ethan finished his morning meal and went out to the stable to borrow a mount. He may as well enjoy a good ride if he couldn't enjoy Brenna's company. He already missed the rigors of ranching, the good honest work that came with caring for the land and the animals. Ethan was not one to sit idly by and do nothing with his time. It appeared he would be in

Scotland for a long while at least, so he may as well gain his bearings.

He rode atop a magnificent gelding, and though to his mind the foreign saddle was not much different from riding bareback, he welcomed the feel of racing atop a worthy steed. The animal carried him over Brenna's green hills, lush with the first bloom of spring. The heavier air enveloped him, and the scent of unfamiliar flora blended with the pine trees. Ethan returned to the lake Iain showed him, dismounted, and settled on a rock near the narrow shore. Compared to the lakes of Montana, this body of water was more of a pond, but it glistened and flowed into a rushing stream. The sound soothed Ethan, and for a brief moment, he believed he could make a home here.

Brenna was in a fit to be sure. She thoroughly disliked spending so much time in her room. One meal could be mildly tolerable, but she wasn't about to spend the entire day alone up there. A step outside on her balcony told her that it was going to be a rare day indeed. The sun peeked through the gray clouds and the fresh air invigorated her. She couldn't ride Heather, but she could certainly enjoy a pleasant walk.

Brenna gave herself a thorough washing and braided her hair to let it fall straight down her back. She dressed in a warm deep-green dress, wrapped her black shawl around her shoulders, and took one last look out her balcony window and stopped. "Iain, you traitor." She left her room to go in search of the old man.

"Now, lass, don't be going and getting upset. It's not good for the bairn." Iain held up his hands and managed not to cringe under Brenna's hard gaze.

"Just tell me why he's riding Crusades." She stood with her hands on her hips, which was a difficult task considering her expanded girth.

Iain shrugged his shoulders before he thought better of it. "That beast is the only one large enough for him to ride. Your man is a giant, lass." This comment earned him a ferocious stare and a bright, red-cheeked blush.

Brenna was mortified to realize where her thoughts had unexpectedly strayed. *One night, just one blasted night with the man, and I haven't been able to think properly since.* "Crusades was Papa's stallion." She couldn't keep the slight quiver from her voice.

"Ah, lass, are ye thinking yer man will harm the great beast? I wouldna have saddled him if I thought so." Iain softly placed a hand on Brenna's shoulder.

"He's not my man, and no, Ethan would never harm a living thing undeserving of it."

Flashes of what Gabriel said describing Bradford James's slit throat caused her to shudder. "It's just that . . . well . . . I don't know." She mumbled and turned, leaving a baffled Iain behind.

Brenna stormed down across the field over her well-trodden path to her special place. The lake gave her comfort so many times before. Not so now. She couldn't move on from Ethan, not with the way she cared for him and certainly not with his child growing within her. Her precious lake glistened under the soft rays of sunshine, beckoning her to sit on its shores and release her sorrows. All she could do was shed the tears her anger would no longer hold prisoner.

"Brenna?"

Why now? She silently cursed the fates that Ethan was here at the exact time she needed to be alone. She wiped at her tears, but suspected he had already heard the anguish of her tears. Brenna lifted her head to look at him but remained sitting on the large stone.

"I'm sorry, I shouldn't have disturbed you."

She shook her head and wiped again at her eyes, this time with a small white handkerchief. "It's all right, and certainly nothing you haven't witnessed before." Except this time her tears were shed for him and not because of the cruelty her grandfather once inflicted. Brenna did not try to push him away when he sat down next to her. His large frame barely fit on the edge of the rock, but there he remained.

"You found my place."

Ethan nodded. "Iain showed me. I hope you don't mind."

"I did when I first saw you, but no, I don't mind any longer." Brenna's gaze swept across the water. "This place is meant to be shared. The others have stayed away, out of respect for me I suppose, but it's not what my parents would have wanted. They took great joy in sharing their life and love with others. I've forgotten that."

"So did I." Ethan set his hand on hers, and she surprised herself by not pulling away.

Ethan sat down at supper the following evening fully expecting to have only Iain for company, so he was amazed when Brenna walked into the dining room. He stood and she nearly took his breath away in her ivory dress and fire-red hair that hung down past her shoulders in soft curls and waves. His gaze slowly moved from her face to her rounded middle and paused. He smiled spontaneously. Ethan couldn't help himself. He felt overjoyed at the idea of becoming a father. He returned his gaze to her face as she sat down, and he found he never wanted to stop smiling in her presence.

Brenna ventured downstairs because she refused to stay in her bedroom one more evening. She thought Iain would keep Ethan occupied throughout the meal. However, when she passed Iain in the hall, he feigned a headache and excused himself. Brenna nearly snorted with that announcement. Iain never suffered a headache in his life.

Brenna wasn't startled to find Ethan already in the dining room, or surprised that he stood when she entered, ever the gentleman, but she was amazed to see him smile when he looked at her. The man actually looked pleased about her condition. It was a thought she didn't want to ponder too closely for fear of being made the fool. They'd taken a step forward at the lake, but their presence together now felt awkward as though they didn't quite know how to take the next step.

Once they'd eaten an appetizing first course of greens and cold salmon in subdued silence, Diane, one of the housemaids, served up roast pheasant with crisp vegetables and sliced potatoes. Ethan raised an eyebrow when he saw Maggie come in and set a large goblet of fresh milk at Brenna's plate, but said nothing. Once Ethan felt confident that the kind, but nosy housekeeper was out of earshot, he turned his attention to the meal and to Brenna.

"I'm happy that you decided to dine downstairs this evening, though I was surprised that Iain didn't join us." *Small talk couldn't hurt anything, could it?*

Apparently not, he thought again after Brenna shot him a quick questioning look.

"Iain's indisposed this evening."

"Indisposed?" Ethan grinned. "Do men get indisposed?"

Brenna couldn't help the smile that formed on her soft lips. "Apparently old men do."

Ethan grinned in response. He'd have to

remember to thank the old man tomorrow.

"You have a beautiful home here."

Brenna looked up from her plate and met his eyes. He sounded sincere.

"Thank you." Brenna wasn't sure what to say when he behaved this way. She remembered once. It wasn't so long ago. *Would it be so hard to remember again?*

"My great-great-grandfather built Cameron Manor. My father made me promise never to let it leave the family." Without realizing it, Brenna brought both hers and Ethan's attention to her present condition and indirectly to them. She cleared her throat and took a long swallow of her milk, but out of the corner of her eye she saw Ethan set down his utensils and face her. She willed herself not to turn into a coward now.

"Brenna." Ethan said in her name in a tone barely above a whisper, and he stood to sit in the chair beside her. He covered her hand with his own, and she didn't pull away. "I said some things when I first arrived that I shouldn't have. Things I didn't mean."

"Ethan, please it's not—"

He placed a finger over her lips to quiet her.

"Just let me say this, please."

She nodded slowly and he removed his finger, leaving her lips tingling.

"I would never try to take our child away from you, and I shouldn't have threatened that. I did mean it, though, when I said I wasn't leaving him behind." She just sat there and stared at him, so he continued. "I'd be lying if I said we didn't need to mend things between us. I was a fool to let you go, but I'm willing to try if you are." He gave her hand a gentle squeeze and let go. When she still didn't say anything he added, "Please just think about it."

Finally she nodded, though neither said anything else that night. Another step forward.

They finished their supper. Ethan excused himself saying he wanted to see if Iain was through being indisposed, though he winked at her when he said it. In a half daze and wearing a bemused smile, Brenna retired to her own rooms.

To Brenna, the next few weeks passed in a blur. Ethan treated her with more kindness than she believed she deserved. She'd been hesitant when he first suggested a walk, but the afternoon excursion became a daily ritual whenever the weather permitted. Iain couldn't feign illness for long, and soon he and Maggie joined them again for the evening meals at Ethan's insistence. The group enjoyed laughter at the table and stories in the parlor.

Brenna continued to grow, and every once in a while she caught Ethan smiling at her with such gentleness in his eyes. *Perhaps we're not fools after all.*

Almost a month after Ethan's arrival, a telegram arrived for Brenna. He didn't want to wake her from her afternoon nap when the messenger arrived, so Ethan took care of it. His insatiable curiosity bid him open the missive, but he wasn't about to snoop, not when he'd begun to regain her trust. An hour later, when she joined him in the library he handed her the telegram, and waited while she read it. The astonished look on her face concerned him.

"What's wrong?"

"Nothing, I think." She looked up at Ethan with an amazed look in her emerald-green eyes. " My brother, Ethan. I think I've finally found my brother."

18

"Where?" Ethan came around her chair. He stood behind and looked over her shoulder at the folded piece of paper she held.

"Kentucky? Ramsey's in Kentucky?"

Brenna nodded. "According to this." She reread the letter once more just to be sure she hadn't missed anything.

Ethan moved around to sit on the chair next to her. "How did you know to look in Kentucky?"

"I didn't. Right before I left Montana . . . " Brenna stopped and chanced a look at Ethan.

"It's all right. Blame for that rests entirely on me."

"That's not true, but we can discuss it

later." She offered him a grateful smile and continued. "I sent out telegrams all over the country. I think the telegraph operator in Briarwood would prefer never to see me again. Anyway, I sent them everywhere, general delivery, and with a note that all replies should be sent here. I also contacted the private detective I used to find my grandfather. He was able search in places the telegram may not have reached." She held up the piece of paper. "This is the only response I've received."

Ethan took her hand, the paper crumbling in their grasp. "Are you sure it's him? It's not his name."

"I'm not sure, but it's my only lead. The person who wrote this letter is claiming to be his sister. The only thing I can do now is write to him there and ask him if he is the abandoned son of a Scotsman with the devil for a grandfather." The laugh that came out of Brenna was unexpected, but she didn't bother to stop it. "What was I thinking? You knew Ramsey, didn't you?"

He slowly nodded. "Yes, but that was years ago and he never claimed or confirmed that he was Ramsey Hunter. I'm sure he's changed quite a bit in those years."

Brenna dropped his hand and went over to the large oak desk facing the window. She pulled something out of the drawer. When she showed it to him, he saw a likeness of a young man in his twenties who looked a little like the man he knew as Ramsey. Ethan looked up at her in question.

"'Tis my father in his twenty-first year. Did Ramsey look anything like this?"

Ethan nodded. "He did, actually. Only I remember Ramsey with darker hair. Otherwise, it's a fair resemblance." He handed the likeness back to her, and she replaced it in the desk drawer.

Walking toward him, Brenna laid a protective hand on her belly. "I'm going to write this Mallory Tremaine. I have to know if I've truly found my brother. Perhaps you could tell me something that only he would know. I just need to be sure."

Ethan lifted her chin with a knuckle until

she looked into his eyes. Without thinking, he lowered his head and placed a light kiss on her mouth. A gentle kiss meant to give support, but it left him wanting much more. He motioned for her to sit down and helped lower her into the chair. "I'll tell you about the last time I saw Ramsey."

Cameron Manor, Borthwick, Edingburghshire, Scotland July 1883

Brenna cursed the gods and mankind for forcing her into this pain. She tried to remember her mother's words and her tutor's lessons when they told her that nothing worth having was achieved without work. *By all the saints, they could have told me the truth—that nothing worth having came without excruciating pain.*

Her screams sounded foreign even to herself. Her only solace was that Ethan suffered with her. She gripped his hand as the next pain coursed through her already ravaged body. No amount of strength she possessed could have prepared her for this. When the worst of the pain passed, she chanced at glance at Ethan. His eyes bore into her, and she almost felt sorry for him. He looked helpless, and when the doctor told him to leave, he refused. Brenna saw the sweat dripping from his brow, and then looked down at her gown, damp and clinging from her own suffering.

"Ethan, go downstairs. You'll know when it's over."

He shook his head. "I'm not leaving. I'm the reason you're in this pain." Ethan appeared by all accounts to be suffering more than she was, though if the increasing pain was any indication of what was to come, she was happy to let him suffer.

Another scream wrenched from her lips, and her fingers tore into Ethan's hand, but she could not stop no matter how much she willed her body. The doctor drew their attention to him.

"It's time, Miss Cameron."

Brenna was grateful to the doctor for he

had not commented once on her single status, and when he was introduced to Ethan, he gave him all the consideration of an expectant father. She bore down once more, and her body seemed to rend in two as a familiar wail reached her ears and her eyes welcomed darkness.

Maggie handed Ethan the baby as the doctor finished up with his patient. The laboring had lasted only three hours.

The doctor rolled down his sleeves and closed his black leather bag. "You'll need to see to it that she remains abed for at least one week. Her body has been through a tremendous amount of stress."

"I'll see to it, Doctor Carson." Ethan held his son and smiled at the doctor. "Thank you for everything you've done."

The doctor nodded, and Maggie guided the man from the room, closing the door behind her. Ethan, now holding his new son, sat in the chair next to Brenna's bed, and stared down at the mother of his child. His love for her only intensified.

After his request that she think about a

life with him, of starting over and mending their hearts, their relationship developed into friendship. When she first went to Montana to seek out answers to her past, there hadn't been time for a proper courtship—everything happened too quickly. They'd been thrown together by circumstance and in his case, by a sense of duty. He didn't regret that time with her, though it seemed a lifetime ago. Ethan wasn't going to find contentment until they were married, and he had no intention of allowing her to slip away from him again. He thought of Hawk's Peak and how he much he missed the ranch and his siblings, but that didn't compare to the love he held for Brenna and the child they made from that one night of love.

Ethan shook his head remembering his departure from home and what Gabriel had said.

"Ethan, if you don't come back with her, I swear I'm going over to fetch her myself and marry her."

"The hell you will, Gabe." Ethan soon realized that his brother just wanted to get a rise out of him and it had worked.

"What are you going to do on this place without me?" Ethan had never been away from the ranch more than a couple of weeks since their parents passed away.

"The boys and I can handle it. Besides, Liza will keep us in line. Hell, what could possibly go wrong?" Well, Ethan had been away much longer than planned and hoped that Gabriel received the letter he sent back on the ship. He'd sent another talking about his plans to marry Brenna, though he'd yet to share the idea with her. He sent only one telegram when he reached Scotland to tell them that he had arrived. Telegrams were too impersonal to convey the depth of what he experienced. The pregnancy he left out, preferring to surprise Eliza and Gabriel with a new nephew.

He stood and placed their beautiful son, Jacob Duncan, into his crib, and returned to the bedside. He lovingly took Brenna's hand in his and lifted it to his mouth for a soft kiss. Ethan smoothed her dampened hair away from her face, and for the second time in his life, Ethan cried. "Brenna, I know you can't hear me, but you have to know. I'm not going back without you. I love you with all of my heart, and perhaps someday you could find it in your heart to forgive me, even if it takes every last day of my existence."

Ethan leaned over her to kiss her soft lips. When he pulled away he was startled to see her eyes open.

"It won't take as long as you think." Her soft whisper did wonderful things to his heart. "I don't know how I could love such a fool of a man, but I do. I loved you from the beginning."

Ethan removed his boots and crawled into the bed next to her, and cradled her head in the crook of his shoulder. He held her as the shattered pieces of their hearts slowly mended. Hurt, revenge, loss—none of those feelings weighed on him any longer. He'd always faced whatever trials came his way and with the life he'd chosen, there were sure to be plenty more. The difference now lay with him. Together, any trial could be overcome and any obstacle conquered.

One week later, Brenna felt fit and refreshed and refused to stay in bed another day.

"Jacob and I will both get sick if we're not allowed to leave this room."

"This should help, Lady Brenna." Ethan slipped a leather sling over Brenna's head to fit on her shoulder and across her chest.

"This is wonderful. Thank you." Brenna held the sling open so Ethan could set baby Jacob inside.

"The Indians in our country use these, but I found a man in your village with the materials and skill to make one." Ethan smoothed the downy hair on his son's head.

"This will certainly help while walking or at the dining table. I have no intention of leaving our son to be raised by another."

Their son. She smiled to herself as she remembered the night she gave birth. It was the night she and Ethan gave in to what they'd known all along—their deep unshakable love for each other.

With each passing day, their friendship and love grew. Brenna believed they were ready for whatever may come. She had another surprise for Ethan but was as yet unwilling to share it. She selfishly kept Ethan and Jacob to herself, until the day came when Ethan decided to change their lives forever.

"He has your hair." Brenna smoothed back the dark strands of feathery infant hair.

"And your eyes." Ethan bent over to kiss Jacob's brow. "He deserves a family, don't you agree?"

Brenna felt her body radiate with joy. "He does, and he has one. A family who will love him all his days and beyond."

Ethan pressed his lips to hers, settling at her mouth long enough to leave Brenna wanting more. He held her hand and said, "It's time we make our family official. Will you do me the honor of sharing your life with mine?"

Brenna would have flung her arms around him if their son had not been in her arms. She knew this day would come, and she never realized how important it had been for them to wait. No barrier of doubt or fear stood between them now.

The week after Maggie allowed Brenna out of bed, Ethan found a local priest. The quiet ceremony was performed at Cameron Manor, with only Iain and Maggie to witness their union. Brenna had been beautiful in a silk ivory dress that flowed over her curves.

"You're even more lovely since you gave birth to our son." Ethan spoke the words only for her and pressed his lips to hers.

"Your family will receive quite a shock when they learn of this." She was now Brenna Gallagher and proud to be so.

Ethan grinned. "Not as much of a shock as you might think. I'll ask Iain to send a telegram tomorrow. I don't intend to leave your side for at least a week."

Brenna held fast to her new husband's hands. *Can I truly be this happy?* She had other expectations for how her life might turn out, but she wouldn't change a single act or outcome, except to find her brother.

Later that evening, she lay in Ethan's

arms, and glided her fingers over his bare chest. The top blanket lay gathered at the bottom of the bed, leaving only the sheets to cover their forms. Their appetites for one another momentarily sated, Brenna's thoughts turned to their child and her brother. She wished for Jacob to know all of his family, both old and yet unfound.

"I would like to reply back to the woman who claims to be Ramsey's sister. I can't imagine why he would be in Kentucky, but it's the only course I have to follow."

Ethan lay his hand over hers and shifted their weights until they faced each other. "We may not find him, Brenna. Are you prepared for that?"

She nodded. "I would rather try and not find him, than give up and always wonder if I could have."

Ethan woke later than was his habit, but he couldn't fault his reasons for a sleepless night. He would welcome many repeats of his evening in the welcoming arms of his wife. A wife who at present was not beside him in bed.

Once dressed, Ethan searched the house, but found no sign of her.

"She's at her lake this morning with Jacob."

Ethan glanced out the window. "I'll join them. She once told me that days this nice are rare."

"Oh they are, but ye can be sure we'll have rain by day's end."

Ethan left the manor without coat or hat, the sun a welcome presence after the days of clouds and rain. He found Brenna on the banks of her lake, staring out to the waters like a woman a deep in thought.

Brenna lifted Jacob from his leather sling and held him up against her chest so he faced the water and the surrounding trees.

Ethan heartbeats quickened. It frightened him to realize how close he came to losing them.

Brenna heard his footsteps before he reached her and turned around to offer him a sweet smile that touched her eyes. "Well, hello to you, Mr. Gallagher."

"Hello, Mrs. Gallagher." He grinned and

put his arms around her and their son. "Do you mind being a "Mrs. and not a Lady?"

"I'm your lady, and only that matters. I'm pleased you've found us. I didn't wish to wake you this morning when the nurse brought Jacob in for his feeding."

"I'm surprised I didn't hear you. I sleep better when you're with me."

"Glad I am to hear you say that, for you're stuck with me now." Brenna cradled the baby in her arms and moved to the edge of the rock. "Will you sit with me? I have something I'd like to discuss with you."

Ethan sat on the edge of the large boulder and wrapped his arm around her waist. "Something good I hope."

"When I came back to Scotland, I didn't realize until I arrived that I left home behind in Montana with you."

He nuzzled her neck and pulled her closer to him. "I know exactly how you feel. Home is with you."

She turned in his arms and placed a half asleep Jacob back in the sling. Brenna's soft hand reached up to his face and stroked his stubbled chin. "I love Scotland, I always will. It's a part of me, and I will miss it."

Will miss it? He nodded, though he wondered what she was getting at.

"I want to go back home—to Montana."

He looked down at her. *Could I be this lucky?*

"You're sure? I'll stay. We can make a good home here in Scotland."

Brenna nodded. "As sure as I've ever been, but I do want to return here when Jacob is old enough, and many times after that. This land is in my blood and 'tis where my parents rest. I want him to see this land, to see where his mother came from and those before her. I'll always carry Scotland in my heart, but 'tis time to go home."

Ethan leaned down and softly kissed her lips. "We will return as often as your heart desires, my love."

Hawk's Peak, Montana Territory
October 1883

One year to the day she had first arrived in Montana, Brenna breathed in the fresh autumn air of the early morning. While her son napped in her arms, Brenna looked ahead of them to the familiar buildings of Briarwood. They didn't want to wait another full day before reaching home, but the night air was too cold to sleep in the back of the wagon.

"The cottage?"

Ethan shook his head and smiled. "I didn't carry the key with me to Scotland, and I don't want to disturb the woman who cleans the place." Ethan nodded to the general store. "Loren keeps a spare room above his store."

Ethan instructed the stagecoach driver to leave their luggage on the board walkway. With Jacob in her arms, Brenna walked alongside Ethan to the steps of the general store.

"Well if ever there was a sight I hoped to see again." Loren ambled down the steps and grasped Ethan's hand. "It's good to see you back home, Ethan." The man chuckled. "Mighty lot has happened."

"It has been almost a year."

"You've brought us back up some surprises."

Brenna held out her son, and Loren pulled back the blanket to look at the sleeping baby.

"His name is Jacob."

Loren stepped back and looked up at the couple. "Your pa would be mighty pleased. Stage came in late today. Will you stay at the cottage tonight? I'd be pleased to join you for dinner at Tilly's Cafe, and I'd be just as pleased to witness her surprise when she's what you've brought home."

"I don't want to disturb Ms. Graves for the key. Would you mind renting us one of your upstairs rooms for the night?"

"Of course I'd mind, but I will welcome you as my guests." Loren called out for the young man who helped him in the store. "Will you help Ethan carry that luggage upstairs?" Loren pointed to the bags left by the stagecoach driver, then turned to Ethan. "If you won't need it, we can keep the larger trunk downstairs."

To Brenna's way of thinking, coming

home had never been such a sweet experience. "Thank you, Mr. B, and I know I speak for us both when I say it would be a pleasure to join you for supper. I can hardly wait to be at Hawk's Peak again, but it's been a long journey."

"Right it has. I want to hear all about it over supper." Loren followed the young man back into the store, but Brenna turned and faced the main street of Briarwood.

"Are you all right?"

Brenna leaned into Ethan. "I'm happier than I ever imagined I could be."

The next morning, Ethan pulled the rented wagon to a halt in front of the ranch house, and no sooner did he jump down, then Mabel rambled out to the front porch and down the steps to meet them.

"Oh, Lordy, Ethan, you finally used that sense God gave you, though I don't know how you found it."

Mabel stopped, one of her well-worked hands pressed against her chest. She walked toward them, her pace slow. She raised a hand to cover a gasp. "Never in my days did I imagine you coming back with a little one."

Ethan laughed and jumped down from the wagon. Brenna handed Jacob into Ethan's waiting arms, but the baby didn't remain there long.

Mabel's awe soon turned to excitement. "May I hold him?" She reached immediately for the baby and gave them her biggest smile. "What's his name?"

Ethan helped Brenna down and slipped an arm around her waist. "Jacob Duncan."

Mabel looked up at them with misted eyes. "Oh, dear." She reached up with one hand and swiped away a fallen tear. "You've done your father proud, Ethan. You've done this family proud."

"I had a little help."

"Of course you did." With her free arm, Mabel beckoned to Brenna. "Come here, child. I might have feared you'd never return, but I saw how determined our Ethan was when he chased after you. I knew then you'd come home."

"And home it is." Brenna returned the

embrace and fussed over her son, who seemed content to remain in Mabel's arms.

Ethan and Brenna laughed in delight as their son smiled up the housekeeper. Mabel mumbled a few more words to them, but it was apparent the newest Gallagher held her complete interest as she carried him into the house.

Once again alone, Ethan turned Brenna into his embrace. "So, Mrs. Gallagher, will you be happy here?"

Brenna eyed her husband and thought for a moment that perhaps she detected a bit of insecurity in his voice. She placed a hand on her husband's chest and looked up into his midnight-blue eyes. "Ethan, my love. Never have I known such happiness. So long as I have you, anything is possible."

Ethan pulled her close and settled his mouth possessively on hers with all of the passion he felt for her. After a few moments he pulled away and looked into those eyes he adored so much. "I think we need a nap." He pulled her swiftly along behind him.

"A nap? Ethan, now is not the time for a . . ."

Ethan turned and gave her a lopsided grin and she gave one right back.

"Oh." She giggled and followed him willingly inside, but they were waylaid at the bottom of the stairs.

"Thought I heard a wagon approach. We didn't expect you until next week."

Ethan studied his brother's red face, and apparent embarrassment. "We managed an earlier train."

Gabriel placed a light kiss on Brenna's cheek and embraced Ethan. "Damn glad to have you back home, Ethan." He glanced at Brenna. "Sorry." Gabriel grinned at them both. "Glad to see the two of you finally came to your senses. I thought I heard Mabel down here with you."

"She's gone into the back of the house. In fact, we have a surprise for you, but first, is Eliza with the cattle?"

Gabriel looked a little disgruntled. "No, because she's not here, and you want to know why? I'll tell you why." He pulled a crumbled letter from his pocket and shoved it at Ethan's chest. With a perplexed look, Ethan smoothed the paper and read while Brenna leaned over to look.

She reacted immediately. "You actually let her go alone?"

"You traveled alone from Scotland," Ethan reminded her.

"I did at that, but I like to believe that if my brother had been there, he most certainly wouldn't have allowed it."

"Now it's not as though Liza gave me much of a choice." Gabriel attempted to defend himself. "She left that letter with a note of her own saying that she wouldn't be away long. She left before dawn. I'm beginning to feel like I'm the only Gallagher at the ranch these days."

"This doesn't say who she planned to meet." *I'm going to strangle my sister when she finally steps foot in Montana. If I don't go and drag her home first.*

"I'm well aware of that. I went to the telegraph office to see what I could find out and who sent it, but the damn man won't say anything. Something about a telegraph operator's ridiculous oath."

"Bullshit." Ethan swore and sheepishly looked down at his wife's amused expression. "Sorry." He leaned down and kissed her wrinkled brow. "But it must be the Tremaines if she went to Kentucky."

"The Tremaine's?"

"Oh dear." Brenna leaned back to look up at Ethan. "You didn't tell them in your letter?"

Ethan shook his head. "Not about that. We have a lot to catch up on."

Gabriel took another folded paper from his shirt pocket. "This one also came yesterday." He handed the missive to Brenna.

Brenna opened the telegram as her heart filled with hope. She felt a moment of disbelief.

Ethan saw the expression on her face and took it from her, then glanced up at Gabriel who just stood there watching them. Obviously he hadn't read it.

"Ethan, it's really him, isn't it?" Brenna sounded almost in awe.

"Really who?" Gabriel peered over the

top of Ethan's hand for a look at the telegram. Ethan saved him the trouble and handed it over.

"You've found Ramsey?"

"It seems so, but this appears to be written by a Nathaniel Tremaine. Didn't you write to his sister?"

"His sister? These are the Tremaines you think Eliza went to see?" Gabriel tried to keep up with a conversation he knew nothing about. Brenna nodded and looked down again at the note. It was signed Nathaniel Tremaine.

"Yes, but how could she have known about them when we only learned before coming home?"

Ethan brought his wife closer to him and lifted her face up with his finger.

"You want to go out there, don't you?"

She nodded absently.

Ethan could tell his wife worried herself over something more, so with a somewhat regretful sigh at the thought of leaving home when he'd just arrived, Ethan offered to go to Kentucky himself.

"No, I couldn't bear to be away from you.

Couldn't I go with you?"

"I could go."

Ethan and Brenna both turned to Gabriel after he made this offer. Ethan knew that Gabriel wasn't fond of traveling, but his brother almost looked desperate to be gone. *Odd.*

Brenna shook her head. "No, you shouldn't have to leave either. I really don't know what to do. A strange feeling I have about this. These people seem to know Ramsey, and this man writes back instead of his sister, if it was his sister. None of this makes sense."

"No, it doesn't."

Ethan frowned over their other problem. He didn't like the thought of his sister meeting up with strangers on her own. He thought, The imp up and left home without a word. For what? To visit a horse farm? To look at new stock for the Hawk's Peak stallions, she had said. Idiot sister. Actually she was one of the smartest people Ethan knew and her judgment of others was rather staggering in its accuracy. *Please let it be with her now.*

Ethan finally relented. "All right. We'll send a telegraph back to this Nathaniel Tremaine. If Eliza did go there, we can hope she'll get the message. As for Ramsey, let's see what your detective can find out about the Tremaines before we make any decisions."

He waited until Brenna gave him her agreement. "All right?"

"Agreed."

"One us of should go after Eliza."

"I mean it, Ethan. I'll go now that I have a place to look."

Ethan considered that. "I don't like the thought of her traveling out there alone, but I don't think chasing her is the answer, and she wouldn't thank either of us for it. We'll have to trust her, and if we don't receive a response from the telegram, we'll ignore what I said and bring her home."

"Ah, Ethan, funny that you should mention detectives," Gabriel said, "but I hired one last month."

"Why did you need a detective?"

"To track down Nathan Hunter." Gabriel stole a quick glance at Brenna.

"Why would you be looking for my grandfather?"

"Some of our boys have noticed activity over at the Double Bar the past few months. No sign of Hunter yet, but it just didn't sit right." Gabriel glanced back and forth between the two, but received no response. "Liza said something strange a few days before she left. It didn't make sense and still doesn't, but I felt we should at least cover our bases."

"What did Eliza say?" Ethan asked with a strong arm around his wife's waist.

"Something about healing old wounds. Like I said, I don't know what she meant, but it's nothing to worry about." Gabriel gave his attention to Brenna. "Being his granddaughter, you had the right to know what I did. I would have asked first but . . ."

Brenna placed her hand on Gabriel's arm and smiled up at him warmly. She always wanted a brother. "I trust you to do what you feel is necessary. And Gabriel? Thank you."

Gabriel smiled at his new sister and was

about to say something else when Ethan interrupted.

"We'll talk more about this later. Now if you'll excuse us." Ethan wanted to drag his wife up the stairs by force if necessary but he stopped in mid-stride.

Ethan and Brenna stood at the base of the staircase and watched as a tall pretty woman with gray eyes stormed down the stairs. Her clothes appeared a bit wrinkled, though of excellent quality, and her golden hair seemed to have been hastily plaited. She held her head high and gave the two strangers a curt nod before leaving the house. She ignored Gabriel who turned bright red, his face looking about as it did when they arrived.

"Gabriel? Who was that woman and why did she look so angry?" Brenna stared after the woman.

"My wife. Sort of."

"Your wife?" Both Ethan and Brenna yelled in unison. They looked to the now empty doorway and back to Gabriel, who looked genuinely guilty.

"What do you mean 'sort of'?"

It was Ethan who had asked that, but Brenna cleared her throat trying to hide her amazement and said, "Well, she's beautiful Gabriel. Congratulations."

Ethan wasn't as pleased as his wife. "You said nothing happened while I was away, just business as usual."

"Yeah, well I may have left out a few things."

"A few things?"

"A lot of things. I'll explain everything, and there's a lot to explain, but you'll love her, I know you will. Her brother, too."

Brenna gasped. "Her brother lives here, too?"

"Well no, they live in the cottage. Actually, they do live here now, but it's not what you think."

Ethan knew there would be time for questions and answers, but with Brenna beside him, and the ranch in one piece, Ethan could find no reason to be angry. "You may want to go after her." Whatever Gabe wasn't telling them, he'd get around to it.

Gabriel raced for the door and left the

couple staring after him.

Brenna still hadn't gotten over her surprise. "He really said 'wife,' didn't he?"

"He sure did." Ethan shook his head in wonder.

"I'd like to help, I really would, but I honestly don't know what I could do."

"Nothing, child, absolutely nothing." A grinning Mabel walked into the hallway holding a sleeping Jacob. "Lordy, there hasn't been this much excitement around here in years."

"When did this happen?" Ethan pointed in the direction his brother and the mystery wife ran. Mabel was the best source of information for everything that happened at the ranch. It seemed he had a lot of catching up to do.

"A few days ago." Mabel grinned, as though unwilling to share the secrets she knew—at least not yet.

"A few days!" gasped Brenna. "Well, they're not off to a good start."

Ethan suspected there was more to it than that, if Mabel's behavior was any indication. "When did they meet?"

"A few days ago." Having piqued their curiosity to the highest level, Mabel began to sing softly as she carried young Jacob back into the other room.

"Yep, not this much excitement in years." She smiled and chuckled softly. Her body seemed to dance out of the room, and holding Jacob closely, a new melody drifted through the air.

Brenna looked at her departing son and then to Ethan. "Should you go after him?"

"Which one?" Ethan shook his head. "Before I left, Gabriel's words were 'How much could possibly happen in one year?' Apparently more than we both realized."

"We both know a lifetime can happen in a year."

He pressed Brenna's hand to his chest and stared at the empty doorway. It remained open, and he welcomed the cool air as his eyes scanned the horizon beyond the walls of their home. Every year this land welcomed new life, but this time, new life had been given to Ethan and his family.

Thank you for reading *Gallagher's Pride*.

Visit mkmcclintock.com/extras for more on the Gallagher family, Hawk's Peak, and Briarwood.

If you enjoyed this story, please consider sharing your thoughts with fellow readers by leaving an online review.

Don't miss out on future books!
www.mkmcclintock.com/subscribe

Don't miss *Gallagher's Hope*, book two of the Montana Gallagher series.

GALLAGHER'S HOPE
Book Two of the Gallagher Series

The story of Gabriel Gallagher and Isabelle Rousseau

From New Orleans to the Montana frontier, enjoy the second book in a series about a family in search of peace, hope, and love on a wild land.

She seeks a new beginning. He seeks what he didn't know was missing. Together they will discover hope in unlikely places.

Isabelle Rousseau must escape New Orleans and the memory of her family's tragic loss. With her younger brother in tow, she accepts a position as the new schoolteacher in Briarwood, Montana. Desperate to keep what's left of her family together, Isabelle joins her life with a stranger only to discover that trust and hope go hand in hand.

Gabriel Gallagher lives each day as it comes, believing he has everything he could possibly want . . . until a determined woman and her brother arrive with a little luggage and a lot of secrets. It will take a drastic choice to protect her and give them both hope for the future.

Return to the beloved town of Briarwood with this frontier romance about second chances and finding love in the face of overwhelming odds.

ABOUT THE AUTHOR

 Award-winning author MK McClintock writes historical romantic fiction about chivalrous men and strong women who appreciate chivalry. Her stories of adventure, romance, and mystery sweep across the American West to the Victorian British Isles, with places and times between and beyond. With her heart deeply rooted in the past, she enjoys a quiet life in the northern Rocky Mountains.

MK invites you to join her on her writing journey at www.mkmcclintock.com, where you can read the blog, explore reader extras, and sign up to receive new release updates.

Discussion questions for MK's novels, and information about joining your book club for a virtual visit, are available at her website, www.mkmcclintock.com.